TO
REMAIN
NAMELESS

a novel

D1602442

RESCUE PRESS

CHICAGO | CLEVELAND | IOWA CITY

TO REMAIN NAMELESS
Copyright © 2020 Brad Fox
All rights reserved
Printed in the United States of America
FIRST EDITION
ISBN 978-0-9994186-7-3

Design by Sevy Perez
Adobe Caslon Pro
rescuepress.co

TO REMAIN NAMELESS

BRAD FOX

a novel

Para la doctora

Only immediate family, the triage receptionist said. Your friend can wait right here. It'll just be a minute or two.

Tess watched Laura about to protest, with her flushed face and heaving belly. How can you argue with a woman in labor?

A nurse stood at the swinging doors, trying to lead her patient back into the examination room, but Laura planted both feet and turned to Tess:

You promised you won't let them give me an epidural, remember? I want to feel everything.—Tess nodded, brown hair falling in her face.—I'm sure I'll ask for drugs. I'm scared and weak, but don't listen to me.

As the nurse started to lead her away, Laura pointed at the piece of paper Tess held in her hand.

I'll ask, Laura said, but you have cotton in your ears. Remember: I want to feel everything.

The doors to the examination room swung shut, leaving Tess under the buzzing lights of triage. She looked down at the paper. Across the top it read *LAURA VALERIO BIRTHPLAN*.

And there it was, item number one: *I am a weakling and a coward*.

Tess laughed out loud as she sought her bearings, alone now for the first time in days. Laura a coward and a weakling. How could she ever believe that? But she'd never felt a labor contraction, had no idea how intense it could be.

She dropped down into a black vinyl chair against the wall. The room empty except for the triage receptionist, now talking on the phone with a big smile across her face. Immediate? Who was more immediate than Tess? She felt the cold, air-conditioned air through the loose shirt she wore. She crossed and uncrossed her legs, head still reeling. She looked down at the sparkling tiles.

Labor, she thought. Now it's starting.

Once in the village above Aswan there'd been a woman in labor, and as they waited for the midwife the woman made such strange noises that Tess walked out into the whitewashed alleyways and paced up and down, stopping in front of the old tomb to ask the dead sheikh what that sound could be.

And now Laura. Laura at 39, who abandoned Tess in the Istanbul office to come back and nurse her own mother on her deathbed, to sit uncomplainingly as her mother wasted away, after working through crisis after crisis, war and famine and bullshit development assignment, now she was in triage, asking for drugs. Give me drugs!

Tess stood back up and took a step toward the door. There was hardly room to pace in here. Her body was awkward and she wished she could be inside with Laura. Wished she knew what there was to do. Wished she'd learned everything there was to learn. What had the Egyptian midwife known? Surely there were things to do in this situation that didn't involve inserting a tube into your spine. Laura had begged her to be here. Laura who had never asked her for anything:

It's a pain unlike any other. That's what I hear. Please be with me.

But I don't know anything about it, Tess told her. I don't know anything.

It doesn't matter. I want you with me. You have to be there.

So she flew from Ataturk airport and landed at JFK and five days later here she was: 7:48 PM, twelfth floor of St. Luke's Roosevelt, just down from Columbus Circle. Five days and it was like she'd been excised from her life, could hardly remember what awaited her: the caseload, the swelling camps, the endless state of emergency. All that was far away and she was here in this waiting room too small to pace in, pushing her knee against the black vinyl of the chair. The triage nurse gabbing away on the phone and Tess could understand every word. Could not *not* understand, really. That was closer to the situation. Back in the US, here in this unfamiliar New York, everyone all around speaking her language. When she landed she thought they must be speaking to her. A colleague or a voice over the phone. *Did you find out where they're being held? And how long is the extension?* After five days she still wasn't used to it. Found herself turning her head involuntarily on the street. Who said that? Who was that? Suspicious, a little paranoid. Relax, she told herself. This is your home country. You have every right to be here. It's important to Laura. And these friendships formed in such conditions, that had lasted this long, it's important to hold onto something. What else did she have? She had to be here, to be a true friend, at least. If Laura was going to cry and suffer and birth a baby in New York, then she would come. Couldn't very well leave her alone. The guy was supposed to be around somewhere but Tess still hadn't seen a sign of him, whoever he was. Laura too proud to push him, probably. But she could ask Tess and she knew Tess would come if she could. And she did. And she had.

But Tess hadn't expected the triage nurse to make her wait here in the waiting room. Just a minute or two. They lie, Tess thought. She listened for Laura screaming her head off in the next room, about to give birth, for God's sake, to bring new life into the world. To add another version of herself. Madness. In this country, empire crumbling, waters rising, Manhattan turned over to bankers and tourists. And this receptionist on the phone. Where did she live? Her slight Caribbean lilt. Parents from Trinidad or something. That melody. People of this city, this hemisphere. Never heard that accent in all the places she lived. Did she ever hear that beautiful Caribbean lilt on the streets of Istanbul? A Bronx accent among the doctors in Kosovo? There was a guy from Harlem in Macedonia, what was his name? Richard Bright, or something like that. Or who said he was from Harlem. Who knows where he was from. A white man from Harlem with his bald head and yellow eyes. With his straight spine and his very correct way of speaking. Flattened, stilted, any character hammered out. Like he'd been printed out or was an iteration of something. Later he said he lived in Utah, or somewhere. Montana. Had moved out west from Harlem to teach survivalism. They were sure he was some kind of agent. Everyone was supposedly some kind of agent but Richard Bright with his survivalism and his hammered-out accent was maybe more likely than others. How long had it taken him to learn to talk like that? Perfectly stilted and proper, and underneath, menacing. Is that how they talk in Utah and Montana?

Back home in Kansas City, her half-brother Max used to tell her about his neighbors in the southern suburbs with their big smiles and their clipped lawns and their children locked up in the basement, body parts buried in the backyard.

Eat the liver, Richard Bright said. If you're trapped in the mountains and the only food is the body of another person, eat the liver first. That's the most nutritious part.

When she met him the way everyone met in those circles, Tess thought he was a horrible asshole. But that didn't stop Laura from going to bed with him. Or had it? His shiny bald head bobbing up and down. Go for the liver.

One thing you could say about Laura. She'd always wanted to feel everything.

Laura had gone from contract to contract, even quicker than Tess, had been at it longer, too. Liberia, Congo, Kosovo, Brussels, Egypt, Istanbul, finally back in New York. And maybe Tess was forgetting something. Certainly she was. What a horrible life, Tess thought. Always in a white 4x4, with instructions to do something that defied common sense and humanity. Always a new language and new geography, new prejudices, new things to be ignorant of. In order to organize the digging of latrines. Pass out plastic sheeting. Source chlorine gas containers. Organize labor. Assess security. Water security. Food security. Public health and hygiene. Food and nonfood items.

Laura was the one assigned to orient Tess when she flew from Sarajevo to Skopje in 1999, the bombs of the NATO airstrikes already falling on Kosovo just fifteen minutes' drive to the north. Laura picked her up at the entrance to H2O headquarters, that huge pink building with its ridiculous columns. Some gangster's idea of a mansion. A provincial gunrunner, sanctions breaker, or something. Now housing the headquarters of an American aid organization, country directors and logisticians and GIS officers. Evil men, Tess thought. Everyone was evil that summer. Except Laura. Who explained the situation and the work to Tess as they drove out to Stenkovec, the first big refugee camp along the border.

They don't want more Albanians to cross over, Laura said, because they're afraid they'll never go home. They'll swell the Albanian population, which is already like thirty, forty percent, and then there'll be a secessionist movement here, too.

Which seems like there already is, Tess said. She'd been following the situation for months.

Laura had arrived a few weeks before from Kinshasa and had no idea about the former Yugoslavia. To Tess it was home. She'd already been working in Bosnia for three years, had flown in from Sarajevo where she'd lived with her brother the last two, before that Banja Luka. It felt like hers by then. Not only her little apartment on Tahčića Sokak, but the language she called Bosnian or Serbian or Croatian depending on who she was talking to, or it was just *your language*, sometimes even *ours*. Laughing at the inside jokes of her Bosnian friends, the bands and movies, remnants of the old multiethnic socialist utopia. Even *Vardar*, the name of the river they passed on the way to the border, she'd never seen it but knew the name from old songs. It was swathed in a glow of associations Laura wouldn't understand.

But all that faded as Tess saw three women trudging up from the edge of the forest toward the razor wire barrier a hundred meters downhill. She watched Laura interrogate the guards at the checkpoint and envied her ability to keep calm as the sullen Macedonians shrugged, and more men, women, and children gathered on the slope.

I should write my questions in lipstick across my breasts, Laura said. Then maybe he'd pay attention.

Tess and Laura were friends by the time they drove back into the city, before Tess started her contract and they were up at dawn to run from site to site through the blazing heat of the summer. Then nights drinking cold wine on the top floor of the house up on Vodno with its balcony overlooking the kidney-shaped pool next door. Sitting there after the endless days, cursing the clenched throat of Tony Blair as he promised more aid. Until the unbearable heat would finally subside under the whir of the Apaches that hovered above downtown.

We should go on strike, Tess said. Tell them fuck your relief budgets, we're not going to fight your war for you.

Laura nodded and smiled as she refilled their glasses:

Exactly. Let everyone starve. Then they'll understand.

It was the first time Tess had been under pressure like that, but Laura had believed in her right from the start—You can do this, Laura told her. You'll be great—when Tess had never seen real conflict before. The Dayton Peace Agreement was already in effect by the time she got to Bosnia. The work in Sarajevo was just pushing through process, return and resettlement. Then everyone rinsing their heads in the basements and bars of the city. But now Tess found herself in a situation that was really happening, right now. Adrenaline shot through her veins as she and Laura raced around in those white 4x4s, out to the camps along the border, kept an eye on the black market networks in the western mountains, occasionally escaping for a mad dash to Ohrid, DJ sets in caves and pink trout flipping in the lake, then in a rush back to the office to grab gear, corral staff, meet engineers, assess landgrades, as fields filled up with more and more tarps and tents.

The backup in no-man's-land, rainfall on fetid corpses, until the borders opened and people came across so fast they couldn't build camps fast enough. Tess ended up in mountain villages, bribing mukhtars to house the overflow. They'd fix the road, build a school, whatever, but please, she said, house these people they have nowhere to go.

Until the bombs stopped dropping and everyone came down from the mountains and the camps cleared overnight. No one knew what was happening, if there would be mines and booby traps. But the refugees didn't care, they headed home as fast as they could, and the camps vacated overnight. Now there were new problems across the border: poisoned wells, unsafe houses, the dead and injured to be tended to, returnees settling scores, vengeance, more killing and confusion.

Max showed up from Sarajevo, Laura headed to Prishtina, and

Tess stayed on in Skopje to administrate logistics. Her boss in DC called in with details for endless invoices.—Sign, sign, sign! he told her. We need to get those supply lines moving!

She signed order after order, huge shipments of lumber and medical equipment and vehicles. For weeks she signed whatever came across her desk.

Sign! her boss told her.

Only when the CIA auditors scheduled a meeting, and her boss's line in DC went dead, did she realize he and the local procurement officer had been collaborating on an embezzlement scheme. Tess was implicated and finally fired because of her signature on all those invoices.—Sign, sign, sign!—The adrenaline now froze in her veins.

As she and Max packed up the house on Vodno, Laura called in on the sat-phone from Prishtina, describing columns of Serb tanks, soldiers flashing nationalist symbols as they paraded toward the border with Serbia proper, toward the small towns and isolated villages where Tess would find her next job. Contracts one after another. Meeting Laura again in Cairo, then in Istanbul where they'd be colleagues in the late 2000s, those murderous years that seem quiet now because they came before all the uprisings.

To be here, finally, trying to stay calm in this reception area. Tess pictured Laura in triage, contracting in front of the doctor.—Give it to me, doctor. Please. I can't stand it anymore.—It had been building up all afternoon. Tess heard her as the sun cracked the blinds early that morning—Uuuuuunnnnh—the winces and moans of pain penetrating her disturbed sleep, curled up next to Laura in Laura's double bed, in Laura's mother's double bed, where her mother had recently died, surrounded by boxes of photos and trinkets, the few things left behind. And now Laura was about to bring a new life into the world.

It's amazing, she told Tess. Life and death and death and life. But I wish my mom could have at least seen the baby. Held it just one time. But no. It was good for her to go. So much pain toward the end.

Now this was a whole new kind of pain, Tess thought. All the period cramps she'd ever complained of. Nothing compared to what Laura was going through.—The drugs, doctor. Give me the drugs!— She pictured Laura sitting on a hospital gurney, hands pressing on her knees.—Uuuunnnh.—The moans and cries that had begun in the morning and grown in intensity through the afternoon. Back in the apartment where Laura leaned over a big purple exercise ball. Squatting over the ball and moaning, her belly hanging low toward the ground and her throat full of those noises, her face far away, or nowhere. She looked up at Tess with her eyes unfocused and her lips just drooping like her belly.

Then all at once it would stop, the strange look on her face would pass and she would be totally normal again.—Wow, that was a good one.—The smile returned to her olive face.—It's so good that you came, Tess. I couldn't do this alone, you know. It's really happening. I wonder if it's time to go to the hospital.

There was a rule: five, one, one. Five minutes apart, they last one minute, for at least an hour. When it got like that it was time to call a cab. Get her downstairs and into a cab and to the hospital.

Oh. Oh. Oh. Please, Tess. Call. It's time.

Tess held the overnight bag they'd packed with toothbrushes and changes of clothes. Also the car seat the hospital had told them to bring in order to take the baby home, which was perhaps the clearest sign of what was happening. The seat that had to be filled. Tess took Laura's arm over her shoulder as they made their way out of the apartment. Stopped in the hallway so Laura could breathe. Waiting for the elevator. Interminably waiting for the elevator, until—ding—they waddled inside and pressed L.

Enclosed in the tiny space. Gravity pulling out Laura's breath. Tess still and calm for a moment until—ding—the elevator came to a stop and in walked a woman and a little girl.

Laura?

Laura turned her flushed and sweating face toward the woman.

Mrs. Lefkowitz.

Oh dear. Are you ready?

Laura continued facing her neighbor, whose face froze in expectancy. Laura's lip hanging, saying nothing as the doors closed and they rode together to the lobby. The doors opened and Mrs. Lefkowitz stalled for a second.

You first, Laura practically shouted, then turned her forehead to the door and breathed while the woman gathered her daughter and moved out of the way.

16

I always hated that woman, she said into Tess's ear as they finally stepped into the lobby. Fake fucking cookbook writer with her recipes.

Out the door and into the cab and the cabbie not reacting in the slightest to the moaning and panting coming from the backseat as he drove the few blocks uptown. The afternoon light as they rounded the corner off 10th Avenue to get to intake.

A moving van backed up, its reverse warning beeping maniacally. Oh, oh, oh.

Until they were out and into the harsh lights of the entrance to Roosevelt Hospital. The guard slouched at his desk. And they were into the elevator, a big slow aluminum-walled elevator and up to the twelfth floor and into triage, to this room where Tess stood now, with her knee against the vinyl of the chair, trying to steady her breath and calm her nerves.

The triage nurse reappeared from the back room, now followed by a woman in a white coat:

Tess?

Yes?

This is Dr. Shen. She's Ms. Valerio's doctor.

The doctor smiled at Tess.

You can follow me, the doctor said. She's been admitted.

And is she medicated?

Lord no, she wouldn't hear of it. I asked her how she was doing, if she wanted to be hooked up to the pain medication, but she told me under no conditions.

The doctor's hospital clogs zigged and zagged as she led Tess down the corridor, her heels suggesting the presence of legs, otherwise unnoticeable beneath the white and green cotton of her scrubs and coat.

The air in the hallway was permeated by an infrasonic thrumming that Tess could feel sharpening and dulling at varying speeds. The walls were hung with photographs of children standing in the middle of a field somewhere, perhaps in India, Tess thought, as vague shapes of forest green and fleshy brown flashed at the edge of her vision.

The doctor was so skinny that Tess wondered how she could deal with these screaming women with their animal noises. Tess looked at her delicate fingers. Like a poet's, she thought. A very tiny diamond ring on her finger. An engagement ring. Who was marrying this elegant black-haired doctor? And would she have babies, too? Tess's head rang with anticipation as she followed, anxious to see how Laura looked now that she'd been admitted, and was without drugs, standing tall, not as weak or cowardly as she'd feared, I guess, Tess said to herself as she followed.

Somewhere down on the street below, just a few blocks away, was the playground on 51st St where Tess and Laura had sat two years before, drinking cans of beer from paper bags, when Laura had just made the miserable decision to move back, to give up her life in Istanbul, her apartment above Tess in Aynalı Çeşme, her job and their work, so she could take care of her mother. It was all she could do, Laura told her. She had to come back. And how could Tess explain or even understand what it would feel like to go on without her? To work and live and wonder where her wanderings and refusals had finally brought her, what without realizing it she had chosen to become.

The doctor paused at the door to the room they were about to enter, her head turned slightly to make eye contact with Tess. A smile, benign and almost sad, animated the lower half of her face. She turned the knob and another temperature of light emerged into the flickering hallway, darker and redder, and Tess could hear groans as she and the doctor stepped into the darkened room. The doctor flipped on a light, and there in the sudden brightness was Laura's naked ass, the big Valentine's Day heart of it, facing her. Laura was bent over the raised hospital bed, with both arms folded under her face, her enormous belly hanging off her torso like one great hardened breast, and as she groaned and twisted her spine this way and that, a large brown hand covered her back, the hand of the delivery nurse, who to Tess's surprise was a man, a heavy man in more hospital greens, who was rubbing Laura's back and pressing down on her sacrum as she rode the wave of another contraction.

That's good, dear. You're doing great.

His deep but somehow ingratiating voice made Tess fearful for a moment. She wondered, startled and confused, if he was the father. How did he get in here while she waited in triage? But no, she shook it off. The nurse. A male nurse. Why not a male nurse in the labor and delivery ward? Half the obgyns were still men.

Oh God, why didn't I take the drugs?

Laura came out of the contraction and rose up from her position, back onto her feet, and spinning around, her face aglow and shining with sweat, she registered Tess and gave her a bright loving expression. The nurse worked a button to lower the bed as Laura pushed her valentine ass up onto it and lay back—Wow, that was a good one—

her face a pale olive turned brown by the sun. The contractions had brought a purple flush to her cheeks and whitened her eyes, and her strawbrown hair fell in tangled clumps alongside her face. Her chest rose and sank and her enlarged breasts pushed through the hospital gown. Laura who had welcomed Tess in Skopje, who she'd sat through the evenings with in Cairo, who'd lived above her in the building in Aynalı Çeşme in Istanbul, whose lustful screams reverberated through the airshafts as Tess lay alone in the dark downstairs. Laura who had spent several months on the border with Syria as the refugee population grew, as the situation began to form in its early stages, only to come back to Istanbul distracted and snappy until her period came.

They're going to let you stay here with me, aren't they?

Of course they are.

Tess moved her still-boyish frame into the room, feeling awkward, gawky, sexless in the presence of Laura going through this, the reddish, beeping room full of machines and monitors. A gurgling, rutting sound surrounded them.—What is that?

The doctor turned her smile toward Tess, eyes twinkling—It's the baby's heart—and put her hand on Laura's belly, showing two large cupped patches under a nylon sleeve that had been pulled around her waist, with wires connecting to a device of some kind, another rack of machines and monitors.

Tess looked up and saw that there was a pair of speakers attached in the upper corners of the room, an audiophile's listening post. She tuned in again to the sound, galloping, as if it were more than one sound, several sounds, beating quickly, insistently, stressed, running after itself. And those sounds somehow existing in a static bath, emerging and mixing with it, static and stress, static and stress.

It sounds okay?

The doctor smiled and nodded her head:

Just perfect.

She said it by stressing the first syllable of perfect, as if she might be mocking Laura, or the baby even, then turned and patted Tess on the shoulder as she walked out of the room.

The nurse followed with his eyes, watched the door shut, then turned to Laura, saying he had to just ask her a few questions. And his ingratiating tone dropped away as he sat at the console to enter her answers:

Was she on any medication? Allergies? Any operations? Serious diseases? Accidents? History of trauma?

Laura wrinkled her nose and told the nurse she was fine.— Nothing like that, she said.

The nurse was satisfied. He pushed himself back from the console and got up.

I'll be back to check on you a little later. And if you need me, just press this button.

He tapped a button next to her bed before heading out into the cold green hallway, pulling the door shut behind him.

Tess and Laura were alone in the room with the galloping sound of the baby.

Can you turn the light off? I told the nurse to leave the light off.

Tess walked to the door and flipped the switch, so the only light was the red-green glow of the monitors, monitoring the quickening pace of the heart as Laura leaned forward and another contraction came on. Tess watched her eyes lose focus, all attention turned inward. The uterine walls tightening, pressing, opening the cervix. Laura emitted low groans. Tess stood up and walked over to her, put a hand on Laura's head and grabbed her left hand in hers, squeezing, letting Laura squeeze, looking down at her friend's face contorted and hurting.

Tess listened to the vacancies in her own chest, wondering what sounds she would make if her uterine walls were contracting, and wanted to crawl out of her skin at the thought. She lay a hand on Laura's sacrum as the nurse had done, and at the same time tried to feel within herself the place where this was happening. Womb. It made her wince.

She had gone astray, she thought, years before. By now her uterus was a chestnut, or a bag with the drawstring pulled tight. And who knows if it was the wars that convinced her, the partition of Bosnia, the assaults on the streets of Cairo, or in Connecticut for that matter. Her fantasies of drone strikes, squads going house to house in Baghdad. Or the brothers who stole rations from the refugees in Stenkovec to sell in surrounding villages, the bulldozing of Sulukule to make way for villas. The smiling voices of American entrepreneurs on their way to the Middle East, worried they'd missed out on Eastern Europe and Russia but now it was their time. It wasn't even some aversion to bloodlust; it was the considered choices, the everyday moronism of the human being that rotted away her fellow feeling. She used to see pregnant women and tell herself they were suffering some kind of infestation.

We should all drop dead, she thought. It would be the best thing that could happen. And as it did, the dropping dead, many times she'd imagined it, the population would lessen until only a few stragglers wandered the planet in an echoing silence and could consider what we had been. Solitary philosophers of extinction. I for one will have no part in our continuance.

Laura was still contracting and her voicebox was stretching and sliding and Tess kept her hand on her back, and felt good to keep her hand there, wondering if it helped. She could feel the warmth from Laura's organism. It helped just that she was there, Tess told herself. The nurse didn't care. Otherwise Laura would be alone in that room, moaning alone, leaning over the hospital bed with no one to steady her big valentine of a behind.

To serve others, Tess thought. To live for others. To despise them, to have been disappointed, and still to work for them. To disbelieve in progress, in benefit, to think that everything backfires. So why do anything?

How was she going to justify herself once this was over? Once the immediacy of Laura's need had passed and she was absorbed into motherhood, and Tess, once again, after the recent bombings, the US launching airstrikes out of Incirlik, had to fly back to her little ground floor in Aynalı Çeşme. Alone, exhausted, recharged, hopeful.

For now: keep her hand on Laura's back, push into her sacrum like the nurse had done. There was no question in that. She savored such moments, when it was clear what she needed to do. Then there was a pure giving that came from her, that flowed like water downhill, and she was the riverbed, and there were sticks and stones but the gush felt good anyway. Laura wagged her ass as she moaned, and it was like sex in a way. Tess could feel it as she rubbed the hard bone beneath her skin, and she thought about the many mornings Laura'd come down from her upstairs apartment and sat with her coffee and told Tess what had happened with one man or another, shaking her head and laughing to herself.

Oh God, but I need them, she laughed.

And now moving her ass like that under the hospital robe, and Tess rubbed and watched her own skinny arms and hoped there was enough power in them to make a difference, felt her own thighs beneath her jeans, elongated, not voluptuous like Laura. Tess braced so she could push into Laura's sacrum—Now they're getting crazy—as Laura scootched back onto the bed—How am I going to do this?—careful not to get entangled in the cords that monitored the baby's heart, still tripping over itself in the overhead speakers, turning the whole room into a womb.

Tess realized she had a bottle of water in her bag and poured some into a paper cup for Laura.

I went to a birthing class, Laura said, catching her breath. My doctor forced me to. The birthing teacher said the pain would find you. You imagine it like an ocean wave, or like a stretching guitar string, or two hands squeezing your body inside, but the pain is a trickster, and whatever you imagine it will find you. It will always be something different than you imagine.

She scootched her ass to one side to try to get comfortable.

Tess imagined the pain like a cartoon demon in red pajamas, a contraction monster waiting for you around the corner as you come strolling, whistling nonchalant, only to spring upon you.

Pain! Hoo-hoo, ha-ha.

Tess sat down and took a drink herself, straight from the bottle, and looked at Laura as Laura looked at the ceiling, catching her breath, with both hands around her swollen belly, tight enough to pop.

Laura with her phone in her hand, checking messages:

Five missed calls. She squinched up her lips and nodded with satisfaction. Hopefully he's in a cab by now.

Who?

Barish.—Tess couldn't believe that after all the years in Istanbul and everywhere, that Laura had come back to New York to get knocked up by a Turk—He says he's on his way—a son-of-immigrants Turk born in the US, who'd hardly ever been to Turkey, who knew nothing about what they'd been through. Asylum seekers, the displaced to the southeast, the dismemberment of their beloved city, seedbanks bulldozed, neighborhoods cleared, teargas and rubber bullets and nights soaked in overpriced booze.

Do you speak Turkish to him?

I do sometimes, Laura said. And he's always like: You don't sound like my mom or my grandma. You sound like the delivery guys at work.

Laura broke out in laughter.

His delivery guys are some bunch of MHP thugs. I've seen the crescents on their truck.

Tess laughed too as she pictured the truck, spray-painted red, three sickle-shaped moons on the side. Just like the flag on the party office on Istiklal, and at marches where the nationalists marched, their double headbutt greeting. Who knew what it meant to those delivery guys, or to this New York Turk asking Laura where she learned to talk like that. Her laughing with satisfaction.

Tess shook her head at the thought. Barish. She imagined his flat head. She was sure he had a flat head. She still hadn't met him, father of Laura's child, would meet him right now in delivery.

Here, when I first came back, Laura said to her. I was at my mother's bedside. I didn't think about anything. But then it went on and I settled in. I started to look up old friends, I started to go out. And I thought: Think about Zeyneb and Arzu and all the Turkish girls who went off to study in the US. They stayed to work for a few years, and everything was going well until for some reason they never seemed to understand themselves they decided to come back. They came back to Istanbul and were happy at first, then started to miss their old lives and only hang out with foreigners. And then they were all, like every one of them: *No Turkish guys. Never again.* I always thought it was funny. But then coming back here I felt like I could understand them. I couldn't take anyone seriously. I was stupid and proud, really. I thought: they haven't been anywhere, haven't been changed by anything, you know?

Tess nodded her head from the big green armchair in the corner, wondering what might ever have changed. In this world where everyone was everywhere, moved and replaced, communicating across distances. It seemed that just to have shared a time with someone was enough. What does it mean, Tess wondered, to have no real shared experience? It's like we're dismembered. Our bodies and minds have long been separated. Now our friends and our memories, the places we live, everything is disconnected and left to drift. I wonder when that happened.

It was also because of my mom, Laura said. It made me feel so alone. And now Barish, a child! Oh my God.

Laura buried her face in her hands.

In the corner of the room was a large complicated device. The nurse had tapped it as he stepped around.—Watch out for the baby

warmer.—It was made of the gray plastic of airplane seats and there across the top was written: *Baby warmer.* A small, baby-sized platform covered in the same blue-and-white padded paper-like textile that unrolled over the hospital bed where Laura lay with her face in her hands. The platform was docked into a wall of controls, knobs and dials, the dormant screen of another monitor. Above the screen was a dark outlet for a hose of some kind, and emerging from the top was a curve of the same plastic material that contained a bowling-ball-sized half-sphere, apparently a lamp, that was the gold color of certain insect eyeballs.

Were you there at the very end? Tess asked Laura, staring at the huge device. With your mother I mean?

Tess was still staring at the baby warmer and for a second had completely forgotten what she'd asked. Somewhere out the back of her ears she could hear Laura's voice, but she was in the frozen, distant place she sometimes found herself. A gray tundra, barren clogged seas, a ringing like tinnitus.— … a whoosh that went through me. I could absolutely feel it.—She turned to see Laura's eyes all red, but from strain not from sorrow. Laura full of baby, who had been describing her mother's death.

I ask her, Tess thought, then my mind disappears. She bugged her eyes for a second. Stay focused.

Laura was talking:

If I think about it there really was something at that moment that passed through me. A friend of mine is a hospice worker and sees people die all the time. He talked to me about it. Every time, he says. Every time I feel it.

You felt your mother's spirit pass through you?

I don't know. But I felt something, magnetism or something. Electricity. I don't know if it was my mother's spirit. It might just have been the spark of her. Like what you hear when you turn a stereo off. Even if there was no music coming through the speakers, you can hear, or more like feel it when they're shut off.

You heard your mother's speakers go out?

Laura laughed a hectic laugh.

Yeah, I guess that's what I heard. .

What does your hospice friend say about it?

Tess scratched her arm. A buzzing swelled quickly in her mind. She blinked to try to silence it.

I don't know, Laura said. I guess just that something happens at that moment. It's *palpable*, he always says, and you can call it whatever you want. He's a Buddhist.

Your friend.

Well, some kind of a Buddhist. He goes to a Zen center downtown, stares at a candle or a white board. He likes it.

You've tried it?

Me, no. There's no way I could sit still like that. But for him it works. He takes care of people dying, and he stares at a white board, and he's happy. He came by all the time when my mom was dying. He sat at the end of the bed and massaged her feet, even when she was unconscious.

Laura lay her head back and both were quiet. It seemed like the first time in hours. Tess raised her arms and let them drop.

That's a nice shirt, Laura said.

Tess looked down at her shirt, some flimsy blue-and-yellow-striped shirt she'd pulled out of her suitcase this morning.

Really? She looked at her skinny forearms. She felt bony and weak and slightly vitamin deficient.

Laura had closed her eyes and Tess could see the contraction coming now, but this time Laura didn't get alarmed or try to stand up. She breathed in deep and slow and Tess stood up idly to walk to her, picked up a hand and held it. Laura made hardly a sound, just the constricted suck of her long inhale, her free hand cupping the underside of her belly. After a long stretch with her face knotted up and her eyes clenched, she released and let out a slight, mournful whimper, then let her face fall to the side and breathed there.

The gold eyes of the future. A gray mist clearing.

The door to the room opened and in came the nurse.—How we doing?—His singsong melody pushed the *we* up high.

Don't be cute, Tess said to herself, or I'll throttle you, watching his plump form as he sidled around the instrument table. There was a rolling chair in front of the monitors, which he slid out of the way with his clogged foot. His clogs were royal blue and his socks were yellow with white polka dots.

He stood over Laura for a second. The baby's heart rate had returned to its normal galloping now that the contraction had passed. The sound of a machine, of a factory. Making baby. Making life. The thing that had whooshed out of Laura's mother had wound up in her belly and was chugging like a locomotive, already attached to a body, a family, a destiny maybe, depending on how you saw it.

The nurse checked Laura's temperature, inspected the spot on her left wrist where the IV entered. The Heplock. Is that what it's called? Why does everything in hospitals have to be so dystopian? The baby warmer keeping watch over us, over Laura draped and chained up in plastic-covered wires.

The nurse checked various feeds, heart rate, blood pressure, adjusted the pads on Laura's belly.

An idiotic stripe of floral-print wallpaper circled the upper part of the walls. A clock. A flat-screen TV in case you wanted to watch TV. In front of the screen were two more insect eyes sunk into the ceiling. Next to the baby warmer sat a rack of instruments, empty fluid containers, tangles of black and yellow wire. A hand sanitizer dispenser on the wall and a control panel called Skytron, with an image of a person alongside arrows pointing in four directions, up-down-side-side, two dials that turned from Low Intensity to High Intensity. A torture device of some kind, it seemed obvious. Two trashcans sat

under a Formica counter. One the same bland color as the walls, the other fire-engine red, marked with the triple crescent biohazard logo that read: BLOOD SATURATED ITEMS ONLY.

The doctor will be in soon to check on you, hon.

Tess looked at the razor line around his hair. The sharp edge above his ear. Tight curls too short to form. Brown skin. Kurdish brown. Egyptian brown. Guatemalan or Dominican brown. The philosophers of extinction walking through abandoned cities would be that color.

Laura's phone buzzed and she glanced at it.

He's crossing the bridge now. Maybe you can meet him downstairs when he gets here.

Tess pictured him an invalid in dark glasses, stepping out of his cab with a cane.

You think he can't find his way up here? We did.

Yes, but you're Tess. He's not. Please.

Tess rose from the chair and thought: Yes. I am Tess. But she was not convinced. She saw herself gangly and not as young as she used to be, wondering what to do with this head full of anger and disappointment, and how she was supposed to be there for her friend in such a situation. Barish with his undoubtedly flat head.

Just tell me when, she said.

But then Laura's toes began to curl and her eyes shut and Tess walked to her and said: Try to get up, I think it was easier that way.

Laura rolled off the bed and again crossed her forearms under herself, and the moans were longer now, and there was a squeal as well, a higher-pitched sound, like it stung, not just the ache like Tess imagined. Tess put a hand on her back again, one on her shoulders and neck, and tried not to think about anything but soothing. She listened to Laura's moans and she breathed long and slow.

It's okay, she repeated. It's okay.

The room seemed redder and darker for a moment, then came into focus. The sounds of the heartbeat quickened, the contractions again speeding the baby's heart. Static and stress, static and stress.

Something else I should do? Tess asked.

Laura was breathing hard as she came back to herself.

Can I have some water?

Tess showed the empty bottle, and the nurse grabbed a bucket off the sliding tray to the side of the hospital bed and handed it to her.

Out in the hallway there's a little pantry with water and an ice machine. Why don't you go fill this up?

Tess nodded and took the thing from him, stepped toward the door and left them both behind.

Tess stepped into the cold air of the corridor with its thrumming. Ice-green stripes in all directions. At the end of the hall, a window. But the window only reflected the cold lamps inside the hospital. Was it nightfall already? What time did they come in? Tess walked with the pink plastic ice bucket. The row of nurse's stations further down was empty. A lone wheelchair turned to the left, as if someone had jumped out and run off and let the thing roll on until it stopped, its nose against the wall. A sign at the end of the hall read PATIENT CARE UNIT. As opposed to what? It was interplanetary. Windows that only reflect inward.

The green is not the same green as before, Tess thought. Each of these rooms is so totalizing that when you step back out you are not in the same world you left behind. When the baby was born and Laura was ready to go, which would inevitably happen, as hard as it was to believe, and they finally open the doors back onto 10th Ave, it would not be the same city they left yesterday, the same world. And not just because of the baby. More because of the inwardly reflecting windows. The baby, in any case, was unreal in her mind. Less real than the sense that everything would be transformed.

Since she was a girl Tess had imagined sudden changes like that: I'm going to go into my room and shut the door and when I open it back up the world will be different. Some other person will be my mother. My house will look different, a different place. What would it be like? A palace by the sea? A tower in the air? Now that she'd been

away so long, it was hard to remember what she'd imagined. What would the name Cairo have meant to her then? Or Istanbul? The spiky skyline with its garland of waters, the last dolphins frolicking between container ships.

To China, to Russia, to the pantry to get ice chips.

There it was. A miserable little closet with a fridge and a microwave, a water fountain and an ice machine with a pile of fresh ice chips in the drain.

Strange, Tess thought, to imagine that someone had just been here. It felt like there was no one at all in the ward except her, except them. Extinction begins now. Maybe someone jumped up from the wheelchair, grabbed some ice and disappeared. Tess looked at the pink plastic bucket the nurse had handed her. It was too big to fit under the spot where the ice fell out, so she had to jam it in sideways and press the latch with her hand.

The sound of ice falling was comfortingly familiar. She could picture her mother who was still her mother, filling her cup over and over again, stirring with a finger, sitting on the cracked leather sofa in the living room of the house where she grew up.

Back out in the false green of the hallway, she stopped to listen, to see whether she could hear anyone else, another woman contracting right then among galloping heart rates. She heard the echo of clogs on tile and voices talking as a pair of hospital staff stepped through from the Patient Care Unit and turned toward the elevators. Then she began to head back to the room where Laura was.

As she walked, remembering the heels of the doctor with her engagement ring leading the way just an hour or so before, she felt a giddy solitude, weightlessness. Odd that it would come over her here. Usually it came over her when she was in a new and strange place, the first time she crossed into Bosnia, that driver with his huge nose. Or

when she first came up from south Serbia to Belgrade when Max got his job there, finding him in that old block overlooking downtown, her asking *What if you died and went to heaven and it looked just like Belgrade?* All those mountain villages they worked in with their ridiculous names: Mrtvica, Žuželjica, Donji Brkovac. That guy who wanted to build an airport in some high meadow near the Bulgarian border, near nothing at all.

After the camps and the airstrikes and coming to see how deep was the corruption of the humanitarian industry, in a way it was good to be in those forgotten corners of south Serbia where no one knew anything and nothing mattered. The wars had calmed. The whole swarm of journalists and crisis junkies had moved on, and she was alone.

And then she pulled into a parking lot in Bujanovac for a meeting with Muslim Relief and there was Abim, his honey-colored eyes and his accented Serbian. It took her a second to realize he was not Rom but a foreigner like her. Tess the Serbian-speaking Amerikanka not as unlikely as him, son of Syrians from the Calle Tobasco in Mexico City.

He made coffee on the electric burner in his office, and their meetings continued until he brought her to his linoleum tile apartment in central Bujanovac. His slowness and ease were all she needed then. Abim in his terrible apartment, as far from home as she was, but who wasn't confused by her attachment to the Balkans and the life they shared there among its last wild peaks.

Max and his girlfriend in Belgrade and her and Abim in the deep south and they were happy like that for a while, like the end of a party when everyone goes home and you're there cleaning up spilled drinks and laughing about who said what. Tess and Abim slept on Max's sofa when they came through, waking up to haphazard breakfasts on the balcony, those delicious cornbread muffins from the bakery downstairs.

Max was always so pleased to have the four of them together. He must have sensed that joyful season wouldn't last.

A morning at Max's, unwrapping foil packages of spinach rolls and making pot after pot of coffee, and Max just back from Istanbul, his first time there, where he'd presented his films and followed Abim's instructions to the dervish lodge in the backstreets of the old city, where Abim had gone when he'd been in Istanbul before they'd met. Max had participated in the ceremony just as Abim had, joining hands and chanting and marching in circles. His scientist girlfriend had mocked him, the glow that came over him, accusing Abim of having converted him. They all laughed then, even Abim, even Max.

It was then that they told Max about Abim's Cairo job—A serious offer, Max. I've got to go—a contract with the International Labor Organization, a chance to leave the provincial projects in south Serbia and head to the biggest city in the Arab world. A UN job. Real stakes, so everyone thought.

A year into the Iraq War. A year after the Serbian prime minister had been gunned down outside the skupština, another flare-up in Kosovo after which some nationalist thugs tried to burn down the last mosque in Belgrade, tossed a pig's head against the front door.

Coming and going from Max's building they passed state security officers in black masks, carrying kalashnikovs. They said their goodbyes over steaming pots of cooked wine, and Tess moved to another country, another continent even, because of a relationship, because of a man.

What a joke, she thought.

Max was heartbroken to have their family separated, but she was happy to fly off with Abim to Cairo. She remembered landing in the middle of the night, the first drive down the elevated highway that winds through downtown. Stopping in the 4 AM traffic outside someone's living room, someone hanging clothes. A universe

indifferent to them. That was the feeling. Everything starting again. The feeling of possibility. It was her addiction.

To think of that here, now, on the twelfth floor of St. Luke's Roosevelt in Hell's Kitchen. American space, as strange as it comes. A bucket of ice. A plastic cup for water.

She stopped for a second and looked both ways, up and down the corridor. The wheelchair rutting against the floorboards. The same sound of air vents and distant machinery. The narrowing corridor, Tess's feet on the hallway's cold floor, forward across the speckled tiles.

When she'd arrived in Cairo she felt like the city would never change. Traffic jams off the bridge since pharaonic times. Abim off to his new job, leaving Tess alone in the tenth floor of the Green Valley Hotel, overlooking Wust al-Balad.

The electrified wail of the adhan, smog in the sky and tables of Ethiopian salesmen down the hall, breakfast in a room with rose-colored windows, burnt carpet, stale breadrolls and white cheese. The grin of the waiter replacing her fork on the frail cloth napkin folded up at her elbow. What did he think?

When Tess took to walking the streets she felt a solitude that was greater in its expanse than anything she'd felt in the Balkans. Alone and suspicious only that she might not have a place here, deserve to be here. What had she done? What did she carry with her? She walked nervous of her pigmentation, her clothes, her height—aspects of life that had never occurred to her in Bosnia or Serbia, where she was easily mistaken for a local—until she learned to forget all that and walk, dissolving into the monsters and miracles of the crowded street, women selling Sudanese cassettes, endless rolls of fabric, tea and coffee and televisions on the street, strains of those melodies, the dark glasses and beehive hairdos of the golden age, the washed-out colors, slate and beige and blue and black.

Om Kalsoum in those images, it occurred to her, looks like Tito's widow Jovanka. Same hairdo.

She wandered and watched until it was time to turn back and

head toward Horreya, that old and vast café with its high columns and half its shutters open to the street, ceiling fans circling slow and steady far above. She found Rasha the tutor sitting with her coursebook opened—*Kullu Tamam!*—blowing on her qahwa mazbut as the lesson began. Rasha in her fine sweater and earrings and composed smile.

Tess was frustrated at first because it moved so slow. She already knew the alphabet, had already memorized 200 words, and Rasha was so meticulous Tess thought she'd never get anywhere. But the *kayf halak* of her studies on the plane was not the *izayyek* of Cairo. Everything was different. Then she heard Rasha's rough laugh and relaxed.

I think I'm ready for a drink, Rasha said, and they moved to the side of the café where the street-facing shutters were pulled shut and blocked, where they ordered rounds of Egyptian Stella out of view of the passersby.

Rasha talked in measured English about her childhood in a compound in Saudi Arabia. Riflemen perched on the surrounding walls. Irrigated gardens, houses straight out of the American suburbs, as if they'd been helidropped behind the wall. Perhaps they had been.

You're always being watched, Rasha said, so you learn to be very chill.

The subject of Kosovo, inevitably, and Tess had never expected that Rasha might have been there. Her stint in Prizren was just research, a way to finish her master's, the practice of resistance or somesuch, something Tess shrieked at, provoking a blush of acknowledgement from Rasha, but still: the Balkans. Tess was a proud citizen, carried it with her. She was not American like the others who came here, who might even believe in the murderous acts of their government.

Yalla, Rasha said, back to 'Arabi.

The thrice weekly, five-to-seven sessions with Rasha always went long like that, until their table was cluttered with green bottles and

the whir of the ceiling fans was hilarious.—Ya Saad!—They called for another.

Then to the buzzing satisfaction of home.

Her years of transience had given her a talent for adopting any room she occupied as her own. The room on the tenth floor of the Green Valley, with its west-facing nook and broken tile floors, nosy staff and lousy breakfast. Soon the apartment on Mahmoud Bassiouny with its lengthening shadows and view of the backs of billboards overlooking the highway, where Abim sat studying or writing up reports or sleeping or cooking. Mexico–New York–Cairo. Egyptian films on the old convex television screen: a fez-bedecked cabaret star twirling his mustache beneath plaster arches and swathes of fabric. Abim at his table or the office or terrible meetings and receptions, the weather unchanging. He went off in the morning and Tess was alone, seated at the table by the window.

She pulled out her notebooks and went over yesterday's lessons, practiced working the muscles in the back of her throat to make the sound of the *qaf*, even though everyone in Egypt elided the sound, passing over it with a marked absence of sound, a glottal stop that was different from the glottal stop of the *'ain*. She turned on the TV and listened and strained to hear the difference, then shut it off and went out into the thick and bright air of the city.

It felt like it would go on for years: Tess stepping alone through the crowded corners of El Hussein or Shobra or Sayeda Zeinab, then back with the rush of traffic to Horreya and studying with Rasha.

After one of their afternoon sessions they jumped into a cab and headed across the bridge to Zamalek, to Rasha's friend Yousry's family apartment overlooking the Nile. Rasha threw herself down on the big sofa, right at home, teasing Yousry's little brother who lay like a lump against the cushions jerking a joystick, manipulating FIFA World Cup

players on an enormous TV, an old bigscreen right out of the American suburbs. Yousry with his curls parted and his sweats seemingly ironed, sprawled comfortably there on his divan, peering at her over a sweating tumbler of whiskey.

This is now the site of the largest CIA operation outside Langley, Yousry told her. So in any congregation of people, of friends and strangers, you can ask yourself: Who's most likely to be a spy? In this situation it's you.

He said it without a smile, not caring if he made her uncomfortable, clear he didn't give a rat's ass whether she was a spy or not.

You might be one and not even know it.

Tess looked to Rasha for support, but she was off somewhere talking to Yousry's sister or mother, who for whatever reason hadn't stuck their heads into that big Zamalek living room.

A spy like Richard Bright, she thought. Would she meet him in Cairo? Would she see him zipping up his fly as he came out of the back bathroom of Horreya, where he would have been trying to chat guys up in the pisser as he'd done in Skopje and Prishtina, hoping to pick up an offhand, unguarded remark that conveyed something. With his bald head and his stiff movements.

Go for the liver.

Tess took her drink and sat at the window of Yousry's living room, looking out at the vast sea of lights across the river and the imaginary movement of its body below. There was reason to despise America, of course, despite Rasha's American accent from her life spent in the American schools of the Gulf. And Yousry's Cambridge English. Did they despise her too? Didn't they have to, fool that she was?

When she left that apartment and walked into a wood-paneled bar full of people in chinos and button-downs clutching gin and tonics, Tess felt like she could have been in south Kansas City. These

people would have greeted her father at his club. Its familiarity was something she never felt in Sarajevo or Belgrade. In the Balkans there was always that heavy accent, either yours or theirs. Everything went across the divide of second languages, and that in a way helped keep you oriented. The challenge was to communicate at all. In this new world the challenge was to keep in mind the possibilities for misunderstanding invited by the fluent English of Rasha and Yousry and their friends. More confusing than the sunken sound of the qaf were these seemingly straight-laced Egyptians who drank Heineken and rolled polite joints on overstuffed furniture.

She gazed at the traffic in the morning, practiced the hard aspiration of the ح and the softer exhale of the ه, pushed air through her half-constricted throat to make the burbling, television-static hiss of the خ, just slightly more pronounced than the Serbian x.

How many times could she start again? Was this the last time? Would she stay in the Middle East, in this world of Arabe-hablantes, until she could roll and laugh naturally in this language?

In the aluminum light of the delivery ward hallway, Tess felt the cold of the ice through the plastic walls of the ice bucket, and pushed open the door to Laura's hospital room.

A carotene tint of scalp through the hairs on his head, the nurse was bearing down on Laura, whose body was all bent up with the folds in the hospital bed. Knees up, back up, hands on her belly, the nurse with his face close to hers, a hand on one of her knees, the other seeming to play around near her crotch.

Tess dropped the ice bucket on the tray next to the bed.

Something the matter?

No, no. Just preparing for a trip to the bathroom.

Tess watched as the nurse reached over behind Laura's right shoulder to where the monitor was spitting out an endless feed of paper covered in jagged lines representing heart rates and contraction levels. He reached underneath the paper and yanked out two gray cables.

The galloping sound halted and silence jolted the room.

Okay, my dear, time to stand up, the nurse said.

Tess backed to the far wall of the room watching Laura struggle to throw her feet over the edge of the bed, while the nurse reached behind her and draped the gray cables over her head so they fell across her left shoulder. The nurse bent down in front of her, pulling little no-slip socks onto her feet.

Laura in a distressed state of semi-nudity looked like a scale model of a person. Her exposed breasts with large, google-eyed areolae, stripped of dignity. Her eyes were still closed, and it flashed through Tess's mind that she'd been raped, that the nurse had raped her while she'd gone for the ice bucket. He sent her out of the room to be rid of her. Her cheeks were hot for a second. And then the thought passed. Absurd streaks of paranoia. Don't be ridiculous. Like you wished she'd been raped. Look at the nurse steadying her as she gets to her feet, doing his job. Always that death-wish, hoping for the worst. And it's only when the worst finally happens that you can relax.

The nurse walked Laura to the front of the room, to where there was a small toilet. He pushed the door open and Laura walked in. Tess could hear her collapse onto the toilet seat and start moaning as the sound of urine hit the water.

Ahhh, aaaah, aaaaaaah.

It's normal that when you urinate, it brings on a contraction, the nurse said. It's helpful.

Laura continued to moan and piss. Then gave a startled yell.

Nurse! she said. There's blood in the toilet.

It's normal, the nurse said. No reason to worry. Lots of things are happening.

Laura got to her feet and made it back into the room. Her face was a mask of concern and confusion. The nurse helped her back onto the bed and she lay back, mouth open and facing up.

The nurse reached over her and grabbed the gray cables, plugging them back into the monitors. Tess watched as the nurse jerked down the pale-blue strip of fabric that engulfed Laura's abdomen. The galloping sound was quiet, and in its place the static was a wash of different beats, heavier and slower.

What's it picking up?

It's mama's heartbeat, he said, patting Laura's chest, who had her eyes shut softly in post-contraction haze.

The nurse moved the gray plastic sensors around until the galloping sound returned, then pulled the fabric band flat, and draped Laura's hospital gown over her again. How could it be a man?

He took a seat at his monitor, entering data.

You're doing great. Just remember: slow and easy breaths. It'll come.

Tess saw Laura open her eyes and turn her head and, when they made eye contact, let out an exhausted smile. She does look kind of postcoital, Tess couldn't help thinking. The look Laura gives a lover after coming back to herself. But no, in that moment she wouldn't smile. Her mouth would hang open. Her mouth would hang open and she would hum from her throat.

The nurse stood up.

You comfortable?

Laura let out a laugh.

You want to turn to one side?

Can I have a piece of ice?

Tess reached into the ice bucket and dropped a sliver into Laura's outstretched palm, but the nurse stopped her from bringing it up to her face.

After this, and he held up a thermometer, which he stuck into Laura's mouth.

Tess picked the ice up from Laura's palm and held it in her own, shuffled it from hand to hand as it dripped onto the floor, then popped it into her own mouth. Laura lay back with the thermometer between her lips, conceding something, it seemed. The nurse went back to his monitor and checked levels. The galloping sound of the heart filled the room.

Yes indeed, he said, you are having a baby.

Laura shut her eyes as a contraction came on.

Oh, oh, help me turn over, nurse, please.

Tess jumped to her feet and the nurse stepped next to the bed— Here—and together they swatted cables out of the way in order to push and pull at Laura's whimpering body until she was on her side, knees pulled up, grunting and crying. The nurse pushed and rubbed on Laura's lower back, and Tess stood awkwardly looking at her burning ear surrounded by tangled strands of hair, walked behind the nurse and picked up a sliver of ice, then edged around to lay a cold hand on Laura's forehead, who responded with a sound that began as a moan and stretched and rose into a tightened squeal.—Eeeeeeee-eh—that resolved into quick breaths, a dog's panting, and then silence.

Tess grabbed another ice sliver and set it in Laura's palm. Laura held it for a second before bringing her heavy hand to her face, slipping it into her mouth, sucking then crunching and swallowing.

The nurse put a hand on her forehead and smiled at Tess before letting himself out.

Imagine we were in Cairo, Tess said. You think they'd let a man be a nurse on the maternity ward?

But Laura didn't seem to care. They were alone again in the room.

When they found each other in Cairo it was the first time they'd met in three years, since those sat-phone calls between Prishtina and Skopje. Now they found each other in someone's apartment downtown. A friend of Rasha's, some globalized Cairene, part of the mini-megalopolis that formed around art openings and experimental music, crowds speaking English and French as much as Arabic. Laura had written a few days before to say she was in town. On research leave from some university in Brussels. Now here she was in Cairo. And with everyone everywhere, Tess wasn't surprised her old colleague from Skopje would show up.

Studies in migration. The Western Desert. Small arms networks into Sudan. Six months at least. Maybe a year. Meet at this party downtown?

Tess had been cornered by a Heliopolitan musician in a Rasta cap and tiny pale blue glasses when she heard Laura's voice, turned and saw her, internally sunlit as ever.

There you are!

You!

Ha. Yeah.

Can you believe this?

Laura told her about Brussels and her fellowship and asked Tess what was up with her, and Tess just huffed and shrugged and said: A spouse.

A spouse. That's ridiculous.

Yeah. We're not actually married, but it feels like that.

She told Laura about Abim, how she'd met him in the deepest reaches of South Serbia, the tiny conflicts no one remembers, spillover from Kosovo.

We stayed for two years down there. It felt like the bottom of the world. Until he got this job at the ILO. So we came here. I mean he came here, and I came with him.

Tess. You went to deepest Serbia and hooked up with a Mexican guy?

That part was much more interesting to Laura than whether or not Tess had a job. And Tess was happy to be able to talk with someone, finally, who knew her. She hadn't realized how alone she'd been.

He's from Mexico City. But Muslim. His family's Syrian.

The Maronites have a big center by my dad's house, Laura said. But I didn't know any of those *Turcos* were Muslim.

And their surprise increased when they found Abim speaking Spanish. They found him in the corner with a woman in an elegant knee-length dress, her spotted neck rising out of a little scarf. Tess waited awkwardly to break in to introduce her friend, Latina también, in a way, at least her father. I mean. Who she hardly talked to, but still. Media Mexicana.

Pues Mexicana, Laura corrected, and told Abim about the house in La Florida she had visited four or five times, and they said a few things about those southern neighborhoods of Mexico City where the Lebanese live. Tess watched this meeting between Laura and Abim and had to scramble to keep up with their banter, which pushed against the borders of her college Spanish.

Abim introduced Adriana, the woman he was talking to, who he'd just met. And she began talking right away, with a guttural laugh and a rasp in her voice and an accent Tess didn't know at the time was

Argentine. Straight black hair and a large mole on the left corner of her mouth, Adriana said she'd just been telling Abim about a pair of Mexican brothers who lived in Cairo in the thirties, Carlos y Rafa, a pair of stuntmen who appeared in old films from the time. She had a collection of photos in her apartment, she would show them.

Laura and Tess left them to move to their own corner where they could catch up and remember the summer of the airstrikes and its aftermath, Laura driving around Kosovo with a mobile ultrasound unit while Tess was tangled in receipts and audits and crooked logistics.

But it wasn't more than a few days later that Tess, Laura, and Abim were ringing Adriana's buzzer and circling up the spiral staircase to her big fifth-floor flat with a view over the endless traffic of Tahrir. Adriana opened the door still wiping her hands and when she kissed them she left a red blotch on Abim's cheek. She moved quickly back into the kitchen and there were plates and cups and cutting boards and where did she get actual salami? She and Abim and Laura chatted in Spanish in the kitchen and Tess looked through the bookshelves of classics and oddities in four languages, then stood on the balcony and watched the traffic until someone called to her and they sat at a big table and ate and talked about the Balkans and Mexico and Laura had just come from Europe and Adriana told them she'd come to Cairo twenty years before with an ex-husband, an Italian beatnik who was long gone.

Poof! She flicked her fingers to illustrate his departure.

She had the calm of a woman whose 55 years had made her beauty more complex, Tess thought, and who would stay lucid and sharp-tongued through many glasses of duty-free wine. When she smiled or laughed she exposed a chipped front tooth and she spoke in a stretched and pulled voice formed in late-night shouting matches. It was as if she had just that second calmed down.

After the Italian, she told them, she married an Egyptian guy, but divorced him, too, and now she was alone in that huge old apartment full of books and rugs and vintage film posters. She raised an arm and splayed her fingers as if she had the power, if she wanted, to halt all the car horns and traffic below.

Turks of the New World and Mexicans of Cairo, Laura, Adri, and Abim formed the Comunidad Latina fi Masr. Adri with the buzzing zh's of the Rio de la Plata and her Cairene Arabic spoken like a woman from Shari' Muhammad Ali. They often ended up at her place on weekday nights, Adri or Abim cooking, eating around the old table bought by one of the ex-husbands, watching shaabi videos and old Egyptian movies—Here's one, Adri put in the disc, where everyone wakes up one day and the great pyramid of Giza has disappeared. Later it reappears, but in Mexico—always talking about the hopeless state of politics, Mubarak, the occupation, the American invasions, the Americans who came to study Arabic now, the Balkans, the growing drug war in Mexico, the engineered crash in Argentina, planes flying out of Ezeiza airport stuffed with cash, the trials of Pinochet and Milošević, Ghaddafi's trip to Belgrade, where he set up a bedu tent in front of the skupština, guarded by his female bodyguards. All those old dictators in their dark sunglasses, the fashion sense of dictators, the wives of dictators, the golden ages of Mexico and Cairo, mustaches and violins, *las dos razas cosmicas*, pyramids, after all, wondering: What could be the Mexican sphinx?

And it was Adri who took them to the houseboat—I have to introduce you!—led them down to the Nile, which disappeared along with the pyramids in the movie they'd watched. The neighborhood was called Kit Kat and there were old movies about that, too. Though there were no movies about Adriana's friend Nasreddin, who she was excited to say was Slovene. Actually a former Slovene, she said. He'd converted to Islam years before and his former Slovene name was long forgotten. He was devoted to a Naqshabandi sheikh, and as they stepped onto the houseboat, afloat on a big pontoon on the river, the sheikh's dry, menacing face looked out from picture frames on the walls and tabletops. Nasreddin's wife Safiya, an Alexandrian with black curly hair covering her eyes, with a paint-stained smock and a beatific smile— What huge teeth she has, Laura whispered—fussed over their twin sons coming on board from the walkway that connected to the banks behind them.

Tess wanted to talk to Nasreddin about Yugoslavia, *od Vardara pada Triglava*, to bond over a shared sense of loss, but watching him as he welcomed them, with his hairless body, pale eyes and white cheeks, patting his sons and handing her a glass of water, she was sure he wanted nothing to do with those times, those memories. It all meant something so different to her, she saw, than it could ever mean to him. So she said nothing, except that she'd been to Slovenia once and remembered the nice willow trees there, to which he screwed up his lips and nodded.

At first Tess liked the way Abim dropped into the cane chair as if he were a family member and asked Nasreddin about his sheikh. But soon they were onto dhikrs and tomb visitations and moulids, Nasreddin talking about *practice*. Tess had never heard Abim say he was looking for a community, as if he weren't content to put his forehead against a plastic mat thrown in an alleyway in Wust al-Balad. Nasreddin would take him to meet his brothers, of course, if he's interested.

Adri and Laura sat on the sofa playing some game with the twins and Tess went outside with Safiya to stand by the water, where clumps of plant-life floated by, huge long-stemmed flowers rising up from green, chest-sized tangles. River hyacinths, Safiya explained, that floated downstream from Nubia and Sudan and Lake Victoria, an invasive species that would eventually choke the river.

She said it with her toothy smile, and watching those clumps of floating stems and roots, Tess thought maybe she felt at home in Cairo. As she remembered the clumps of garbage and dead animals that floated down the Sava in Belgrade, she thought maybe she could forget about Yugoslavia like Nasreddin had. It was just a transitional step on the way here. To this houseboat on the Nile, to Adri's fifth-floor flat, to the tables behind the closed shutters of Horreya, to Abim and Laura and these new people.

Her chest filled with carbonation for a moment. She could feel it rising up to her shoulder blades and her neck. And with Safiya's shining teeth in her mind, Tess thought the huge viral flowers added salt to the beauty of the place, the movement of the river, a constant that ran beneath the unchanging course toward dissolution. Man and Nile, Mexico and Egypt, Buenos Aires and *aguas amenazadas*.

She'd been on her way here since she left home at 21, hitchhiking northeast to New York to visit Max, who she found in a heroin-infused haze on Attorney St. Since she flew to the H20 training camp in Italy, naive enough to think that humanitarian work would edify her, would distract her from her own problems. Since she sat up in Banja Luka with Katarina, who'd escaped the massacre in Vukovar, then in Sarajevo with Azra and Max, so many laughing nights. Until she'd grasped something of what it meant that Yugoslavia, that old country she'd clung to, which had formed her, where her friends had grown up, that nonexistent place with its old movies and songs and stupid jokes, was gone—Poof!—like Adri's ex-husbands. Everyone had scattered, died, stayed, returned, rebuilt. The world was new for them, too, and Tess was part of that. And then Max came to live with her and they floated from Sarajevo to Skopje to Belgrade, sometimes together and sometimes separate, family in a way they'd never been when they were young.

Those years infused the way she saw Nasreddin, as she turned to see him still deep in conversation with Abim. Who knows how she'd have seen all this otherwise. Maybe there was something in the loss of his native country that had driven him here. Maybe one day she would ask him. For now she stood with Safiya, happy to look out at the river. She was a clump of biomatter like the water hyacinths, traveling downstream, washed up here, atop this pontoon on the Nile.

She heard Abim calling to her, saying he had to get home. There were emails to answer, another week of work. The employees of a garment factory in the Delta were on strike, and the ILO had taken up the issue. He had to prepare for a trip to Mahalla where he would talk to the workers and make a report. The report would then disappear into the ILO void and nothing would happen, but that was the job. Nothing happens, but at least it takes you places. Meetings, reports, correspondence. While Tess would wake up and look through job listings, feeling unqualified for anything with her rudimentary

Arabic.—No one speaks Arabic, mi amor. Remember how it was in Serbia.—Which she knew of course, but she hated the fools who came to Bosnia or Serbia without a word of the language; she knew that they knew nothing, that there was no way for them to know anything, that the structure of the international community was intended to keep them stupid, to make it easier to shove uncomfortable policies down everyone's throats. That's why the OSCE rotated their staff every couple of years, to maintain the stupidity and dependence of their staff. Tess was not going to be a part of it, she'd find something else.—Okay, that's fine, mi amor. But I have to go take care of a few things before tomorrow.

She said go ahead she'd catch up, then watched him walk off the houseboat onto the shore and disappear toward the bridge to Zamalek, his loose curls and his skin.

Soon they all decided they'd better leave, Adri to her place behind Tahrir and Laura to the apartment she'd just rented in Garden City, and Tess told them to go ahead, too, that she wanted to walk, that she felt good walking, so they jumped into a car and she headed down the darkened sidewalk alone.

Crossing the bridge she felt her moment of happiness evaporate as fast as it formed. What was she doing? Where? Why? Nothing ever got better. In Zamalek she passed the flags and signs of international organizations, the international community having descended on Cairo along with the spies. Worse than spies, she thought, the internationals damaged and distorted and imposed their own banality and cowardice on whatever they touched. Best to leave things alone. She had already seen that in Serbia. Don't touch, don't touch, you know not what you do. So what to do?

I love you, a man said to her in English from a street corner. She tensed for a second, but noticed with satisfaction that she had succeeded in not looking his direction. The women behind trellises. Watch what you wear. She had tried to ignore it at first, but no. It was a fact of life here. She covered her shoulders, changed the way she dressed. She wanted to disbelieve every western cliché, oppressed women in headscarves, all that, but she still didn't make eye contact. Wouldn't in New York either, but even so, it was different. Or that was just how she felt. She didn't know. She'd grown up at a time when the McFarlane gang ran crack at the edge of her neighborhood. Drive-by shootings and police raids. Bodies in boarded-up houses. Why fear an Egyptian trying out three words of English? But she still trained her nervous system not to respond to the calls and whistles and songs.

A taxi slowed next to her, honking its horn to attract her attention, following her as she stepped toward the next bridge. She stopped, turned away, said nothing, walked up a side street and continued on Ahmed Sabry, then after a block or two returned to the avenue via Brazil St, under the overpass and across the bridge.

I love you, she repeated to herself. I love you I love you I love you.

When she got home Abim was at the round table in the living room, blue light of the screen on his face, and she sat to practice her words and grammar: alif ba ta tha jeem ha kha.

Abim off to research the strikes in the Delta, then to the poor Coptic neighborhoods south of downtown. Afternoons in Horreya and nights with La Comunidad Latina. The sense of Cairo as a teeming, expanding, opening creature. The wash of traffic beyond the billboards, orange light and brown dusk.

At night alone with Abim in the apartment, eating fool-ta'miyya from the corner and watching the glow from the silent television, showing another old Egyptian film where a poor man who struggled to survive ironing shirts for his wealthy neighbors, through tricks of fate and misunderstandings, rewarded for his buffoonery, ends up mayor of the city.—May I become poorer! he sings to the foreign woman in the nightclub, who bobs her head back and forth as if she's listening to an old jazz number.—May my enemies become richer! he sings, prompting the backup singers to chime in: May we be his enemies!—The lifted eyebrows and bugged eyes of the acting of that time. She could hear them in imaginary English: *Well I'll be!* The curly arches of the stage sets, the thin façades of the city streets, when outside now they heard the rush of cars, horns and engines. Abim on his back on the sofa, watching idly as Tess rolled a cigarette, then set it down without lighting up. A long, easy moment of nothing-doing. His chest rising and falling, pushing up his right hand draped across his chest.

Tess wondered if they'd grown closer since they'd come here, wondered what was happening to them. For two years they had lived together between Vranje and Bujanovac in South Serbia, and back then it was like they were the only people alive. Abim with his village councils, interethnic dialogue, funneling Muslim Relief to the Albanian population that spilled over from Kosovo. Tess shepherding small projects in the most isolated villages of the region. Traveling up lonely peaks deep in the Balkan range, then back down to their polyurethane and cinderblock apartments, to the strange life they formed together, a relationship that grew strong because it grew slow and easy, in isolation, and in a way Tess had never experienced, without rushing or fluttering or frantic pushing or pulling. And there he was now on the sofa, raising and lowering his right hand with his breath.

Threads and needles, the tightening knot of veins at the back of her eyes, like a stinging veil over her vision.

When he turned his honey-colored eyes to her they were warm and didn't judge her the way she judged herself. She walked over and sat down on the cheap carpet thrown over the planks of the floor, so the back of her head pressed against the side of his ribs, and he began to stroke her hair.

In the morning Tess ran into Safiya on the corner, coming from a meeting with a gallerist downtown.

I need to go buy some fabrics, she told Tess. Let's go.

It was the first time they were out in the city together, now walking up Talaat Harb to the roundabout. Safiya had been patient with her on the houseboat, and informal, almost flirtatious. She touched Tess on the wrist when she spoke to her, and squeezed both her hands when they said goodbye. It was good to see Safiya's buoyant nature out in the city, to be in her company, to sit and walk and ride with her. They passed the metro station and walked along the avenue with its rolls of industrial carpet and textile. When they crossed, Safiya took Tess by the crook of the arm before she moved into the traffic. She did it thoughtlessly, but Tess felt a pang of gratitude. It was good to be cared for. They turned down into the smaller streets as they approached the old city, past shops of old toys and electronics, repairmen, small squares with piles of wooden slats and furniture on the sidewalk.

In Alexandria, Safiya told her, there's a market called Crowding Women Together. There you can buy all kinds of beads and fabrics. But here: everywhere I look there are shops like this one.—She came to a stop before a storefront display crammed with mannequins dressed in red and blue silks, teddies and push-ups and gartered stockings.—Shall we go in? she giggled. And Tess felt unsure how to respond, watching the women in black—Rasha called them crows, but Safiya never did— as they huddled through the door, each pushing gently against the black cloth of the woman in front of her, to enter and fling aside the doleful material and be free among rhinestone bras and whalebone corsets. Tess wondered what would happen if she went in with them. Would they strip her naked and dress her in red and blue silks? Safiya and Tess frolicking among torn-up feather pillows, giggling with these women, sharing their secrets the way women can when they're alone together, when they've always been alone together.—Come on, Safiya grabbed Tess by the crook of her arm once more and led her further down the alley, where they came to a corner with a few tables and sat to drink lemonade and tea.

Particles of dust and car exhaust and human skin suspended in the thick solution that was the Cairo air.—Mmmm, this lemonade is delicious.—Tess relished its sting. The lemonade maker had peeled and blended the little green-yellow fruits whole, rather than squeezing and straining them, so all the rich bitterness of the rind was there too.

She slurped the lemonade and wondered at the huge teeth of Safiya when she smiled, at the black smock that at home on the houseboat made her look like a painter, but here in the market made her look like just another woman. Except she wasn't, Tess thought, and none of the other women were either. Each one in black and drab and gray smocks and dresses, some with heads covered, some with faces covered, some in trousers and dresses and jeans, were also not the women of the market, were not Egyptians. They shared nothing except the fact of being crowded together here, like her, in the thick polluted light that made the air seem still and the seconds syrupy, and even if they didn't throw off their smocks and frolic among the feather pillows, there was a kind of solidarity in it.

She finished her lemonade and dropped the cup on the table. It looked like an Old Fashioned glass, like a glass like she'd get if she ordered an Old Fashioned at Milton's Jazz 'n' Juice on 39th St back in her hometown, sitting with Max on one of his visits, or her sister before she left, times she would never have imagined how far she would go, how alone she would be, or that she would ever feel a solidarity like this. If she'd ordered an Old Fashioned at Milton's, even already then, it would have come in the same glass her lemonade came in, sweet and powerful as it was.

After an hour or two Safiya had an armful of fabrics stuffed into plastic bags and they jumped into a cab in front of one of the gates of the old city and returned through the traffic and over the stultifying bridges to the Kit Kat waterfront, where they sat outside on the deck of the houseboat drinking tea and talking until it was night and the men still hadn't come home from wherever they were.

Do you ever go with him? Tess asked.

No, Safiya answered. It's not for me. He's sweet to me, I don't have a problem with him, but the Qur'an is always telling men what to do with their wives. It isn't addressed to us. For him, though—and she shrugged her shoulders, laughed, and stood up to say goodbye to Tess, squeezing both her hands before Tess turned away.

Tess again walked across Zamalek back to Wust al-Balad. Tonight no one bothered her or told her they loved her. She walked peacefully, feeling at ease even with the fact that Abim who did love her was somewhere chanting and breathing and repeating la illahi illa allah over and over again, crowded together with men she knew nothing about and would never meet or understand.—May they become richer!— She could not even understand what it meant to Abim, only that it shone in his eyes, all the prayers he'd said, or at least she imagined it did, and that was wonderful in its own way, too. It was wonderful not to understand, to be alone like this, really alone on these streets after a day with Safiya crowded together with the women, with the rush of the Nile all around her. And she ought to go home and look through job advertisements but instead continued down Talaat Harb to the Stella Bar, with its blacked-out windows, where she hoped to find Laura seated somewhere over a green bottle of the unexceptional beer that they watered their nights together with. But Laura wasn't there, she was somewhere else, either at the Greek Club or back at Horreya or at Estoril or at home or someone else's home. Tess considered looking for her like she had on other nights, to find her upstairs at the Greek Club with a bottle of White Horse whiskey in a paper bag under the table, talking about Mexico with a perfumer from Lebanon, but instead Tess sat alone at the Stella Bar and ate the crackly roast beans from a bowl and drank her beer quickly before anyone spoke to her, her scruff of brown hair hanging over her forehead as if that were enough to disguise her, then got up and walked out without looking at anyone, headed quickly back to Mahmoud Bassiouny in order to get there before Abim did, crawling in as he would smelling of the sweat of strange men, and as she walked she felt like someone who had stolen something, or been forced to admit a lie, and had to get home quick before anyone found out.

Uuuaaaaooonh.

Laura's moan grew until it swallowed the room, and Tess's hands of their own accord moved to press into sacrum, rub lower back, to bring warmth and relief, and she moved her body into the pressure, too, leaning in, curling over. It felt good. It felt good to do it.

A weakling and a coward, she thought. How can you not love her? Her face closed up and purple like a prune. More like a ripe plum.

The contraction passed and again Laura was calm and lay on her back on the hospital bed, her knees up and her arms at her side, palms up, fingers gently curled, neck flushed and eyes slightly clouded, taking shallow breaths, washed in the sound of the baby's heart, which continued to patter insistently in its aspic of static.

It's like death, Tess thought. This process. In and out.

Species, subspecies. They were at sea, far from shore, afloat somewhere. The lights of the West Side out the window, all around them, the distant yellow lights of anonymous apartments. They were nowhere. On a distant planet, alone in the interplanetary space, that lonely darkness, the sea of darkness when there is no moon. The interlunar sea. Afloat there somewhere. An infinitesimal speck moving off into the distance.

Did your mom ever tell you about when she gave birth to you? she asked Laura now that she'd recovered. Were you in New York?

No, they were in Cuernavaca, with a midwife.

In Mexico?

Yeah, back when my mom was going to be a painter. They rented a house in Cuernavaca from some family friends of my father, and they spent two years there.

Tess remembered a picture of them, from the collection of photos Laura had put together when her mother was still alive, an attempt to keep the dying woman's mind active. Brought her stacks of prints to show her, the white borders of the sixties and seventies. Now in a shoebox in the closet, which Tess had pulled out and flipped through back in the apartment. She remembered a shot of Laura's parents in Mexico. Laura's father a dark-haired man in a pale yellow suit, and Laura a bundle of cloth in her mother's arms.

She stopped painting because of you?

No, she painted all the time, even after I was born. Mostly street scenes around Cuernavaca. But she couldn't get over her northern melancholy, so even the mercado looked like an Edward Hopper diner.

Tess tried to imagine the taste of the fruit. Avocado and mamey and guava that tasted like 28th and Broadway, like the East River or the D train. Like Laura's hair.

I don't remember anything, but I went back later and I recognized the main square from the one painting she kept.

The one in the hall. I know that painting. The sepia fruitstand.

The saddest one, Laura shook her head and smiled. But yeah, I was born in the house they rented. Just my mom and dad and the midwife, a woman from Cuernavaca, or somewhere. She kept soaking towels in steaming hot water and packing them around my mom's belly. And she kept telling the midwife: Make them hotter, make them hotter. The midwife had to keep boiling water, and my dad could hardly touch them to pack them on mom's belly. He never let her forget that, as if it explained something basic about her. *Never hot enough for that woman!*

Laura shook her right hand in the air as she imitated her father's voice.

Now she checked her phone once more, then lay back and rested quietly with her eyes closed.

Time for me to go down? Tess asked.

But Laura just shrugged and said nothing. The contractions had exhausted her, coming on for most of a day already, and she lay on the hospital bed in the darkened room and rested her eyes, her mind covered in hot towels, her chest rising and falling like Abim's on the couch in Cairo, rising and falling, enswathed in the sound of heartbeats through the speakers, the trail of numbers coming through the feed, into the monitor and output in red and black digits above the bed.

The numbers: 85, 88, 82, 90.

When the contractions came the numbers jumped past a hundred, two hundred. Now they rested, even if the sound was still quick and relentless. It was consistent for the moment, and Tess might have grown accustomed to it, though that was beside the point, really. The pain monster wasn't lurking around the corner to pounce on her, after all. The pain that would come for Laura no matter what anyone did. Laura without drugs, left to feel everything, a coward and a weakling. Tess was happy to be the cotton in her ears, the matchsticks keeping her eyes open.

It was a wonder she could lay there so peacefully.

Tess felt her own body again as she slumped into the plastic chair, the fold in her belly that made her frown at her posture. Her arms were warm with effort, somehow, from rubbing Laura's sacrum, supporting, massaging. The wear felt pleasant. She could feel the circulation in her palms as it pulsed against her cheek.

She turned to look out the window, looked past the reflection of her face into the lights of Midtown. The cliffs of Manhattan outside, the anonymous towers. The weekend she spent with Max here, some fifteen years ago, before she left for the first time. And for good, it seemed by now. Of course she would come through, like now, but to live? She couldn't imagine. Maybe she sensed it even then. Walking around downtown as it was then. A cop riding an electric cart, like a golf cart or something, down Attorney St, chasing the drug dealers who used to hang out there, who Max bought drugs from, back when there were still drug dealers on the streets of Manhattan.

From the hospital window the city looked mournful and lonely, like the fruitstands of Cuernavaca as painted by Laura's mother. Anonymous money-hustlers in midfloor apartments, overpriced and locked in. Down on the streets the city scurried with action and promise, but up here it was just the yellow lights of hallways and bathrooms, the blue flashes of a television in the larger windows of some living room, a person sitting alone, eating carryout. The television lights themselves were from another time. No one even watches television anymore. Those old TVs had disappeared with the drug dealers, maybe. In Cairo they used to sit TVs on plastic crates on the street corners, and men would gather smoking shisha as the footage played, old movies, old concert footage, the news with the sound off. Shisha smoke, the clatter of dice and murmur of conversations, an occasional slap of palm against tabletop, the place you go at the end of the day. Like Horreya or Estoril or Stella Bar became for her. The only places in town, for a city that size. You were always sure to know someone, which made the city, as vast and monstrous as it was, intimate. Too intimate sometimes. No one out the windows of midtown Manhattan had a place like that. Or even wanted one, maybe. The streets with their air of impending events. In Cairo the syrupy seconds promised always more of the same. One day bled into the next, never rushing. An explosion in the market, somewhere, and then the stream of tourists quieted for a month or two. A concert at the university where you saw everyone you know. Fifty protestors in the square surrounded by hundreds of security officers. The upheavals to come were impossible to imagine. It seemed like it would always be like that. Cabs backed up on bridges would honk until the end of time. Meanwhile five to seven with Rasha, tenses and declensions, then at the table at home to look at job listings. Months of fruitless job searches, studying with Rasha and sitting with her friends until she didn't feel ashamed to try to speak Egyptian. Still, she applied for work so half-heartedly, she assumed, everyone must have smelled it on her. Some despair about human effort already ingrained in her. What could she possibly do here that would be worthwhile? Perhaps Cairo encouraged that. Or encouraged her to feel that way, brought it out of her. What do you do? Finally she met an editor at *al-Ahram Weekly* and he began to give her articles to edit. It was enough that she was a native speaker of English, she could rewrite awkwardly translated sentences, sentences written in someone's second or third language, and with that she could at least feel that she wasn't freeloading off Abim. Sometimes the articles had to do with his cases: *Textile Workers Strike for Bonuses*; *Garment Workers' Sit-in Reaches 26th Day*; *Women Workers Speak Out*. Incredible to think anything could come from this, she thought, then chided herself for thinking that, then corrected the sentences and pressed send and went to Horreya to meet Rasha. Went to Adriana's, went to the houseboat or the bar. Sat on the floor of the apartment on Mahmoud Bassiouny and let Abim stroke her hair, felt his hand on her neck, the pale fur on her neck rising with mixed feelings. Laura in the Western Desert. Laura in Suez and the Sinai. Populations in movement. The traffic on the bridge.

She stepped onto the houseboat to hear Abim and Adriana talking to Nasreddin outside on the deck. In the living room she noticed a copy of the Qur'an next to the twin's school notebooks, thought about Nasreddin teaching his sons to read the Qur'an. Something about that idea: this man from Ljubljana, a middle class ex-Yugoslav, not even a Balkanite, really. Just a European, a white man with white cheeks. She thought of the Bosnians who'd found God on the battlefield. But it wasn't that, either. Not at all. How did he find his way to Safiya? Tess had only been to Ljubljana once, the swampy little Baroque center with its weeping willows drinking from the river. How does she understand him? A convert in a way that made him different from Abim. His faith required a deliberate change of identity. But who was she to say what we were and weren't allowed to do? Who or what we could become? What if we don't like who we are? Surely she could understand that.

She found Adriana on the wicker sofa with her shoeless feet pulled up beneath her, fondling the string of little amber beads with silver fringe Abim usually carried in his pocket. Lately when Adri talked about him, when she mentioned his practice or his progress—*el morir antes de morir, escapar hacia arriba*—the swoon in her voice began to grate. Abim whose religion had calmed Tess in the south of Serbia, whose patience had broken down her alienation. Something about living in a Muslim country made it different. It was no longer a secret, the way it was in Serbia, even in the southern oblasts where the Albanians lived. Here it was everywhere, the sound was everywhere, in every taxi the slurred old cassettes of recitations. Plastic mats unrolled, women through the other door, the red eyes of the sheikh that shone from the walls wherever she looked.

Tess hemmed and sat and listened to their talk. But when her phone buzzed and it was Rasha, Tess said sure and excused herself and headed back to the rush of traffic along the sidewalk, across the bridge to Zamalek.

She met Rasha and Yousry in the back of a restaurant, darkened walls and colored lights. Yousry had traded his ironed sweats for a cashmere sweater, a sign of occupying only air-conditioned spaces, the ultimate luxury in Cairo. Never to be in the heat and dust and smoke and chaos of the street. Tess thought there must be some subtle chemical effects of such an existence.

But for now Tess ordered a drink, lit a cigarette, and fell into their banter, describing the scene she'd just left on the houseboat.

He's becoming like one of those foreigners in India, Yousry said with a laugh. They disappear up into the Himalayas and come back with matted hair and stinking like the devil.

They used to go to Benares, Rasha joined in. Now they go to Sayeda Zeinab and El Hussein.

For these two, who had spent their lives avoiding sheikhs and imams, blocking out the sound of the slurred cassettes of the taxi drivers, nothing could be more laughable.

With Abim in his researches and Laura hemmed in by deadlines, Tess settled slowly into the circles of Rasha and her friends. Abim could huff and chant and interpenetrate with the divine for all she cared, she would drink bottles of Stella in Horreya then blow the smoke of Sudanese weed out Yousry's window above Zamalek. No more alleyways behind El Hussein, what seemed to her more an indulgence in the supposed exotic, fleeing from oneself. She preferred to sit in the sophisticate trappings of Yousry's Cambridge education, ancient Cairene pedigree, and foppish, connoisseurial entourage. His groomed sarcasm and Rasha's sloe-eyed reticence. Their laughter was light but constant, Yousry's shoulders rising and falling without a sound as he described the clerk at the phone shop.

You know the dot on their forehead they get from pressing their noses to the rug? This one had three?

Yousry's brother stared insistently at the television screen. Just like a boy in a suburban house outside Chicago or Boston or anywhere.

I bet he rubbed his head back and forth until it bled. That's what they do, I swear.

Without their cynicism, maybe, or their indifferent acceptance of Tess into their banter, having forgotten to ward her off with half-hearted anti-Americanisms, perhaps she would have found a way to be in Cairo somehow, maintained her awe of it or her foreigner's sentimentality about it. She would never have been able to conceive of the city as home, as it was to Rasha and Yousry and their friends. Whatever longing and desire she had felt, what made the city magical, evaporated above Yousry's brother's joystick. The Nile, the markets, the crumbling buildings, even the camel drivers around the pyramids became ordinary to her slowly, sometimes hilarious, reminding her unjustly of the fake Spanish architecture of the Country Club Plaza at home in Kansas City, where tourists from Omaha and Des Moines came to go shopping. The architecture and texture of Cairo was the backdrop to someone else's childhood and adolescence. Rasha's and Yousry's and others she slowly got to know.

I'm lucky, she told herself, that this is not the first place I came to, or I could have been fooled into identifying with it, like she had for a time in Bosnia, in the ex-Yugoslavia. The thought of Nasreddin when he arrived in Cairo, of her in Sarajevo. Now I know better. I'm immune to identification. Like them: she watched the television lights reflect off her friends' English spectacles as they jabbed dumplings from the Korean food brought up by the delivery guy.

She thought of Abim's amber prayer beads with their silver fringe, him buying them in Khan al-Khalili. He isn't dislocated like me, she thought, but striving for a past that may or may not open to him. She remembered him walking back onto the street swirling that string of beads around his fingers. Like a boy, she thought, like a teenager who wants to be Humphrey Bogart. It was an amber glass of whiskey that turned out to be filled with sand. She walked home with her head full of smoke feeling free of all that—*But God knows best*—imagining Nasreddin as the fool of old stories, riding his ass backwards on the way to some ritual or other, leading Abim somewhere she couldn't follow.

And when he came home in the early hours, his eyes more transparent than ever, smelling of tea and men's sweat—Hey, mi amor, I know you're in there—she held still, not wishing her solitude to be disturbed. It was good to be alone, she thought, rather than pretend to relate.

I know you're in there, Abim said to her closed lids. And despite herself she rolled over and sought out his compact frame, his smell that lingered beneath the tea and sweat, the smell she had come to take almost as her own. How could she feel distant? She eased her mind into remission and felt her body. Her skin came alive again and her muscles ached with pleasure, her belly dropped down into itself. Afterward they lay staring at the ceiling, and their separation was tangible, a third person who had gone into the other room for a second, but now was back. She spoke to no one, to the ceiling, to Abim:

It scratches, she said. But it scratches a place that doesn't itch.

70

Through the windows of the taxi, Barish watched the lights come on along the West Side Highway. The honey crickets were out, hopping here and there. The blue-gray aluminum of the Chelsea Piers, a smudge on the window distorting the scenery. Bicycles and joggers, a blur of headsets and workout gear. Muscled forms in skintight textiles. Mostly just necks and midriffs bouncing along. Early October, which he'd always thought of as the most beautiful time of the year. Now it would be associated with the road to birth of child, his last cab ride as a free man. The sun had just set and night was forming quickly. Fall was in the air, but the warm weather still felt like summer. Free and flush. A bee boo bah. There was no reason to worry. When he saw it he would know. People made a career of worrying. Not Laura thank God, which gave them a chance. Maybe it wouldn't be an exhaustion of tirades and incriminations like his parents. He could only ever be himself anyway, so might as well get used to it.

The cabbie was African, Senegalese probably. A skullcap and a dangling sura from the rearview. Must have kids of his own.

He imagined himself in an afternoon reception hall, setting up for an event. Servers and security. Married? Some guy in a suit asks, normal as can be. Got kids?

Yes sir, a bright son. Just turned five. Gonna start first grade. Seems to have a good throwing arm. Kicks a ball like you wouldn't believe.

Pffffffft. People don't even talk like that anymore. Co-parenting, baby yoga, lessons in Chinese.

He rolled down the window, took off his glasses and wiped them on his shirt. Exhaust smoke blew away the lemon scent of the vehicle. Too bad you can't smoke in the cab anymore. Used to be there was nothing like a cigarette in the back of a cab. I would move to a city where you could still do that. Not even Istanbul, says Laura. Where can you still smoke in a cab? Argentina? Probably not. China? Probably only in some godawful country where everything smells like shit and exhaust and then you don't even want to smoke anymore. Suck in the air. That's good enough.

Barish pulled out his phone and looked at the messages.

Baby! It's starting. Meet us in the hospital. Ack you!

He smiled at Laura's energy. Her sweat-streaked face after sex, her hungry mouth, strands of beautiful greasy hair in her eyes setting off the warmth of her skin.

Had they never decided what night it was? Or morning or afternoon? Cold winter night. With the poor woman dying in the next room. Shut the door and keep it down. Trying to stifle their laughter. His penis slides in and boom! straight into the future. Her eyeballs pop right out of her head. Her breasts swell up and he sucks mouthfuls of milk. She screams and laughs and scratches and in the next room the poor old woman suffocates on a teaspoon of saliva. Will always suspect some act of reincarnation. Laura giving birth to her own mother. A sad and solitary woman who gave birth to an irrepressible spirit, a force of nature. Only to have her squirt out her own melancholy baby. *Squirt*. What would it be? Funeral baby. Mourning baby. End of a perfect fall day, sunset over New York harbor. The glinting Hudson in the falling night.

What if I see that old woman's eyes in the baby? Or my own grandmother dying confused in Chicago. But when she was young— talk about honey crickets.

The cabbie turned off the highway into Hell's Kitchen, the vehicle slowed and they were back on the Manhattan streets. Barish had served cocktails at a place along this stretch. Lecherous bald Turk for a boss, who only hired East European girls and told them they were Ottoman subjects. His huge hairy ears.

You could birth an eye or an ear. A wise old man in a baby's body, who will look right through you, who will know your secrets and your faults and who you'll have to bow down to.

Father, bring me sucking tool! Baby commands in a thundering voice. *More of hum hum sugar candies.*

A cigarette on the step of the Grolier Club, where she was keeping watch on some guy who was exhibiting a cache of her mother's papers. Letters of the Mexican Boom.

What was she? Barish had asked, incognito in his catering manager's formalwear.

Nothing, Laura said. A scholar. But she must have had some power over them. Because they all wrote these letters to her that really sound like love letters. Though she never admitted anything with anybody except my father. Not that my father cared one way or the other.

He passed her a cigarette and was happy to smoke with her in front of that hateful building with its sniveling managers and dowdy old ladies, pretending they know something about poetry because they spent ten thousand dollars on Ezra Pound's shopping list.

A sinologist of milk and a quarter-classicist of eggs.

Squaawk.

After their fourth drink, after making out in the bar, by the time they got in the cab he had already half-lost his footing, but she brushed her hair out of her eyes and sat calm in the back of the car, cracked the window and watched the city go by, holding his hand in some way that told him to keep away for the moment, let her be alone like that. They would have their night but for now tranquilo, hombre. And he understood and knew she appreciated that. That was their moment of understanding, so that breakfast the next morning could only be laughter. And he thought: maybe this is just what it feels like.

By the time the old woman was in the coffin, they figured out later, she was already knocked up. But they didn't know that at the time. Very soon. Really like the day she died. It must happen like that. Things happen like that. She didn't feel bad about it. Never felt conflicted about going into the next room when the old woman breathed her labored breaths, eyes glassed over. There was only one way she was going. Now this.

Say goodbye to the carefree days and years. The late nights with no one to call. The playing it by ear. The nothing and nothing. Turn off phone and walk through streets unreachable. No one knows where I am. The grateful afternoon before a shift, or a day when there's no work. Showing up unannounced. Poof. Let it go.

When the river flows backwards and the morning follows the day and the clock strikes three hours for every minute and the grandmothers are born of mother, of babies of mothers, mothers of babies.

Look, man.—The cabbie pushed his wallet through the opening to the back seat, a photograph of a child. A boy, Barish guessed.—My wife gave birth right in that seat where you're sitting.

When they pulled to a stop, Barish handed the cabbie two fifties and told him to keep the change.

For good luck, he thought, as he pushed the door shut and looked through the glass panels into the hospital emergency room.

Another moan and Tess was hovering near the ceiling, watching herself massage Laura's back until the door opened. A slice of cold light from the hall and the voice of a man.

Laura fell back on the bed, exhausted, not even attempting to say hello to Barish as he came into the room.

His voice was textured like tree bark, and when Tess turned involuntarily, she was surprised to find his head covered in salt-and-pepper bristles. His skin was freckled and his features looked both sculpted and soft.

He walked to Laura, put two palms on the side of the bed and said nothing for a second, then lay a hand on her forehead and began stroking and smoothing her tangled hair. Laura returned his gaze with an unfocused, spooked expression, and they looked at each other in silence.

Ocean liners and seafront weddings, tables set with cutlery. A wainscoted parlor where men sat ignoring their card games.

Tess moved to the side, watching as Laura's eyes came into focus. Was there love in them?

Not a chance, she thought. It was something else. Awe. Not at the man but at life. At how far away she could be from the urges inside herself.

Then she propped herself up on her elbows, saying: Tess, Barish. Barish, Tess. And Barish turned now to face Tess. He was in some kind of button-up shirt-jacket, some senseless thing made of gray canvas.

Wasn't the light designed to resist these interruptions?

Barish chuckled slightly from nerves. He went to take Tess's hand but kept his arm low and his elbow bent, so they stood close to each other.

Politesse, she thought. But disengaged, abstracted. Maybe a hash-head, maybe a solitary whose reins were so loose he took everything as if it just happened to be.

Tess nodded to Laura, who was looking at the ceiling.—She's doing great.

His head was not at all flat, of course, but pointy. Her Belgrade friends would undoubtedly have called him špicoglav. The point aimed back, a rounded perch as much as a point. You could rest your thumb on it. What will it be like to give birth to a little pointy-head baby? With his overgrown eyebrows. Ataturk eyebrows, Laura would say.—Will our child have little Ataturk eyebrows like you?—And some perfectly decent, mesomorphic build. Spoiled, no doubt, Tess thought.

He began to speak in his treebark voice, at first Tess just heard the sound and not the words, about his cab ride and his work and how he was trying to get there as fast as he could, and he'll always remember because the cabbie pulled out photos of his own children and was describing his trip to the hospital the first time with his wife. Harlem Hospital, her water breaking on the way. New York brotherhood.—Finally, here I am.

He had a big natural smile and cocked his head to the right slightly.

His accent was one hundred percent American. It hurt Tess's ears. Why should an American accent come from under those eyebrows? At least a little musical Turkish warble. But no. Laura. Always thoughtless.

I told you Tess would be here, she said. Remember? My oldest friend.

Which was strange, because it felt like they had met at the end of the world, and that they were already very old when they met. She got to Skopje, to that border crossing with Kosovo, the banks of the Vardar. Everything had already happened when they met. What was any of that? How could she be her oldest friend? But by now yes, it must be true. Who else could it be?

Tess had her face turned toward the particle tiles of the floor, began wondering at the straightness of the pattern they formed. Was it the same all through the hospital?

Laura squinted and said: Wait here it comes, and began to try to stand up. Barish was right next to her but stepped back, not knowing what to do.

Tess just sat there.

Help her up, she said. She wants to stand and face the bed.

But then Tess saw the cords that led to the heart monitor start to wrap around Laura's arms and neck. She sprang to her awkward feet and pulled the cords up and over Laura's head as Barish steadied her, the moans coming as she turned. Laura crossed her arms—Move, Tess said to Barish—and lay her forehead over her wrists—Oh God, said Laura—and Tess shouldered Barish out of the way to press on Laura's sacrum, all of the sudden sure she knew exactly what to do— Like this, she showed him, who stood close by but didn't know where to put his hands.

For a second Tess and Barish were both holding their breath and Laura let out a long undulating sound. Barish now put a hand on the back of her mess of hair while Tess held her hips.

UNNNNNnnnnnnnngh.

Time was suspended and the air temperature rose and fell. The static and stress of the heartbeat sped through the room, a space capsule hurtling through space, propelled by Laura's moans.

Then they stopped, and Laura uncrossed her arms and pressed on the bed and pushed herself up, supporting herself on her palms.

She got back into the bed, lay herself back, and as if in preparation for something, everyone went quiet. The heartbeat quieted too. Into that steady galloping darkness, the door flew open, and there appeared Dr. Shen.

She was backlit at first, her white doctor's coat aflow as she emerged from the imaginary green light into the warm darkness of the delivery room. She looked for a second like a gunslinger entering an Old West saloon, as if her doctor's coat might be made of dry ice, shards of light refracting off the diamond on her long, delicate finger.

Laura was lying peacefully now and Barish was teasing her— No, you look beautiful. Look at you—and he continuously smoothed her tangled hair back from off her face until her eyes grew larger and she did now, really, Tess had to admit, look beautiful, flushed and radiant. Tess sat in the chair by the window and looked past them to see what Dr. Shen would do.

Hello, family. How are we?

That singsong voice that only exists in America. But Dr. Shen wasn't like that, she was serious and straight to the point. Tess watched as she perched one half of her minuscule behind on the hospital bed, peered into Laura's eyes for a second then turned to Barish, who had moved out of her way to stand by the baby warmer, next to the red bin with its biohazard sign.

This must be the father.

Hello. He wrapped his arms around himself and nodded to her.

It's getting stronger, doctor.—Laura struggled to prop herself again on her elbows and a strand of hair fell over her face.—It has to be soon.

The doctor shook her head mysteriously, then put a hand on Laura's thigh.

Laura threw her head back and made a long moan.

Just remember to breathe deeply when the contractions come. It's like a wave crashing over you, you can't resist it. You have to just let it come, crash over you. It comes and goes.

Oh God. Laura screwed up her face in pain now. Her cheeks rose and wrinkled. Her eyes were nowhere to be seen. Tess watched her clutch at the mattress with her hands.

Just breathe, just breathe.

I can't I can't I can't aaaaahhh no I can't.

The doctor made a blowing sound, like a long smooth exhale.

Ah God stop doing that I can't do it I can't do it.

Barish was still leaned against the wall, just watching. Tess grabbed at Laura's hand, but Laura pushed her away.

Aaaaaahhhhaaahahaa.

The doctor just kept making the blowing sound and Laura kept moaning. Then the moaning subsided and the doctor stroked her arm, saying: That's good, that's very good.

When the doctor got up and left the room, the nurse followed her, remembering this time to shut off the lights, and again they were hurtling through space in the darkness of the room.

Is there more of that ice, Tess?

Tess found a few slivers swimming in the melt. Barish grabbed the bucket from her and placed a couple of ice bits in Laura's outstretched palm, then flicked cold water on her face.

Ah, ah, yes. Do that. Do that.

She closed her eyes and pushed out her face against the droplets released from Barish's fingers. He stuck his hand into the melted ice and lay his palm on her cheek and forehead and Tess watched her purr in pleasure, her neck contracting and releasing, contracting and releasing.

Laura in her mother's apartment doing the dishes and sweeping the floors. Laura bringing bottles of Vouvray from the shop in the ground floor of her building. Laura in the Kurdish poet's café, when he brought out plates of white cheese and little sardines and they talked about the Van earthquake, about her last visit to Diyarbakır. Talking to everyone always, fearlessly and with that warmth and flush that now shone on her cheeks going cool from Barish's icy hands. It was still her, somehow.

The many afternoons and evenings, especially evenings, when Tess grew tired of walking and wandering and grabbed her little flip phone and Laura answered out of breath, just coming in the door.—Perfect timing. I was just coming in the door.—Always like that, like she knew. So Tess made her way from the honkings of Tahrir to the curving streets of Garden City and found Laura thrown back on the sofa with the windows opening onto the backs of buildings along the Nile and the sun between them, dropping over Giza.

Laura's skirt bunched up underneath her, her face turned toward the ceiling until she propped herself up on her elbows to ask a question.—You want to go?—Then getting ready and in a car to the south of the city, to a party, another friend of Rasha's, someone connected to the Romanian embassy. They were expecting the diplomatic scene, some version of it, but when they emerged out of the staircase onto the terraced rooftop they found a bunch of US Marines around a table. Big guys with consolidated energy, not laughing, passing around bottles of booze. Amazing how young they are, Tess thought, how familiar.

Well, look at this, Laura said, stepping around them to where another group stood at the edge of the roof. They found Rasha there leaning against the short wall that lined the terrace, talking over her beer.

I ended up at a military party in Kuwait, she said, visiting a friend in high school. You had to watch out. They were naval officers. They'd been at sea.

Laura laughed.

You had a good time, come on.

Yeah. You know we actually went off with a couple of them.

Rasha spoke slowly, with half a smile on her face.

We snuck onto a ship in the harbor. It was empty. My friend said it had been sitting in the harbor for years. We were out there, smoking weed, and I didn't see it, but an ember must have fallen into a fuel canister or something, because there was an explosion.

Rasha's hair fell into her face for a second, as she turned her chin down, and a laugh broke through her dark voice.

I have no idea what happened, actually, but I'm standing on the deck, the city behind me, and then flames started to shoot out from some vents on the ship, and then the whole thing was on fire. We ran to the shore and hid, still completely high, and the guys ran back to wherever they were supposed to be. We never saw them again, but we went back to the harbor and watched the flames eat up the ship. There were other people there too, watching, and we sat near them. They had no idea it was us who caused it.

Tess watched Laura watching Rasha as she laughed, the three of them together on that rooftop. She'd been in Cairo long enough now that these friendships had started to deepen. She savored Rasha's laugh and her deceptive calm; she knew it well. Something new was forming, like it had in Skopje and Sarajevo and Banja Luka. She thought of Katarina who had first housed her in Bosnia, who had taught her the language, initiated her into declensions and old TV shows, the local brand of bullshit, even found her the job in Serbia later. Katarina who had escaped a dark basement beneath the Vukovar massacre—*Mixed marriage, not wanted anywhere*—with her black eyes and her dimples and her deep and forceful voice. Tess knew she could call at three in the morning and Katarina would drive across the country if Tess asked, no question. Friendships forged in the Balkans, she thought, like with Laura. Rage and despair and loyalty cooked into them from the first moments. Perhaps it was the same with these soldiers on the roof here in Egypt. Combats troops in Iraq, no doubt. On their way to or on the way from?

Rasha was looking at them too, thinking her own thoughts about them.—I want to ask them what it's like to participate in a war crime, she said.

The electric light of downtown, Tess thought, the rooftop, the city, the month and year and day, even, it was all contaminated. The marines and her and her friends, too. Tess pictured people from her heartland home, wondered how often they thought about Iraq, whether they knew that its poison was in their food, their parents and children. The big invasion, just four years ago but like it had been decades, released a noxious cloud that grew and spread and upstaged the stink of the Balkans. It was obvious to everyone that the invasion, the occupation, whatever it was, would never end. It had started and it would go on forever. It was in her and in Laura and Rasha, too. She remembered Katarina who she left in Belgrade for another job, another city. A few days before she left, Tess and Katarina saw footage of crowds in Baghdad pulling down the statue of Saddam Hussein.

No one loves you anymore, Katarina had said, using the collective pronoun *vas* that meant Tess, too, was part of it, part of being American. Tess had to live with that the way Katarina had to live with being a Serb, no matter the bombings and marches and her Vukovar basement.

Katarina was the first person Tess called after protestors drove a bulldozer into the national TV in Belgrade, the chaos that led to Milošević captured and sent off to the Hague, those few days of celebration. Katarina said it was like you'd been drunk for ten years and now finally started to sober up and look in the mirror and could see what you'd become: youth annihilated, home and country, any sense of innocence, belief in human goodness.

All those years, Katarina said, you knew you were okay because at least you weren't that guy, you weren't Arkan or Mladić or any of the petty criminals that went down to shell Sarajevo or go on raids in Kosovo. So then you didn't have to worry about yourself, what you did or who you were. If you were in Belgrade you stayed out of the way, away from the cops and criminals, holed up with small circles of friends in little bars in empty shopping centers, in the little tugboat on the Sava, anywhere where you were likely to be left alone. And then it was just day by day. Bad affairs, hilarious drunken and drugged-out nights, dissolving into the pit of the past, half-remembered, minor scandals between friends, one day after another. Everyone degraded, banging their heads against the wall like children, but somehow good, at least not like *them*. Now that was over, the dictator was locked up, and you were left to realize that you'd aged ten years, hadn't studied, hadn't learned anything useful, just survived, and that was enough to break your heart.

Now with the stink of the US in Iraq afloat through the rooftops of Maadi, and knowing that this would go on for years, had already been going on for years. And Tess remembered telling herself: Don't forget. Don't let them distract you.

But distract you from what?

Back with Laura on the sofa in Garden City, Laura's skirt bunched up underneath her. The intelligence that gathered in her cheeks. Laura knew as well as anyone that any data she gathered, the shipments of small arms through the Egyptian desert and Sudan, the communities displaced from Nubia, from the areas affected by the race for resources in the horn of Africa: it would disappear into the oblivion reserved for studies and reports.

No illusions, Laura liked to say.

Tess believed there was a scar left on everyone who passed through the Balkans, on her and what she thought of as her generation, anyone who had participated in the supposed relief effort: a fleck in the eye, a reminder that nothing is going to get better, that any attempts to help will only be perverse, unproductive, antiproductive, and finally, absurd. There were those who fell in love and who stayed on made a life for themselves, but most moved on to other lives. Like Tess and Laura here now, in Garden City. But the scar was there too, that fleck in the eye. So Tess wanted to know what the intelligence in Laura's cheeks could offer. Or her own. What were they distracted from? From Serbian and Arabic and new people and cities to explore and discover. Populations in movement, the traffic in the city, circling and circling around Tahrir, which they crossed daily, the many lanes of traffic, as if they were about to be squashed like the frog in that old '80s video game, not imagining what was soon to happen in that place, only to get to this apartment in Garden City, curving lanes with little gates here and there designed by the English to prevent insurrection. The light over the Nile, and the years between them.

To sit at the table finally, drink tea or Egyptian wine, joke about the news, about the people they knew, about a situation with a traffic cop that afternoon, what he'd said to Laura.

He'd stopped traffic, she laughed, saying *How can I work when I'm staring at the moon?* All those Arabic poems about a woman's face like the moon, those clichés.—I mean, he really said that. A cop!

She could always come here to Laura, and that was good. As long as Laura was in town, or around, as long as this situation lasted, which it wouldn't go on forever, of course, for any of them. Not being able to predict where they would be in a year, if they would still know each other, be in touch. For now they laughed through the afternoon light. Orange orb falling through the pollution across the Nile. Chemical fumes rising up from the buildings, the towers and apartment houses, all somehow the same color, the same color as Belgrade and Sarajevo, too.

The day of Laura's deadline, she submitted her study of small arms networks and came right to Adriana's, stepping inside carrying a bottle wrapped in paper. Tess closed the door behind her as Adri, white apron wrapped around the pale blue shift she liked to wear at home, her feet in terrycloth slippers with little pom-poms flying here and there, scampered across the floorboards to see who Tess had let in, taking the bottle and putting it in the freezer. Old cumbias bounced off the Egyptian film posters on Adri's walls, among them an image of Carlos y Rafa, the Mexican acrobats she first mentioned the night they all met. Their illustrious predecessors, she said. One of the brothers was flying through the air, tucked into a ball, and the other stood below, gazing up with arms outstretched, a striped jersey tight around his muscled chest, about to catch his brother. In the space between them the Egyptian deserts, a small pyramid on the horizon.

Tess found Abim out on the heavy masonry balcony overlooking the traffic. He asked Laura what's next for her now that her stipend was set to dry up.

Anything, she answered. Reliefweb listings, querying thinktanks. There's a post-doc in Berlin I should apply for. I'm always surprised any of those programs still exist. Sit in Berlin and research and study. Wouldn't even have to know German. But I got a response just now for a job in Istanbul, so maybe I'll go there.

Tess shouldered up behind Abim, taking one of his Cleopatra Lights from the faded gold package. His next trip would take him back down to the Delta to check on the strikers. Had labor conditions improved after a year?

You ever thought to go to school, Tess?

But Tess just shrugged: migration studies, peace and conflict studies, area studies, Islamic civilization. *Women Workers Speak Out.*

I'm heading up the Nile, it looks like.

Tess had received a call from an old colleague from Macedonia, a Brit who'd worked for DFID and remembered her. All of the sudden there were possible consultancies, paid for and organized by others. Assessments, reporting assignments. Someone to go somewhere and say what's going on.—I just need someone I can trust, Tess.—And she'd said yes, fine. Which meant that she would be off working somewhere too. To go, to see, to file a report. Sent here and there faster than ever before. What would it lead to? Would she end up somewhere, confronted with something she couldn't yet imagine, but that would change her, bring things into focus, expand her ideas of what she was capable of? She remembered the night she and Max spent sleeping out on the Acropolis. They'd left Skopje and Kosovo and the bombings and camps and headed to Greece, only to be struck by an earthquake. Everyone in Athens was afraid of aftershocks, so they spent all night on the Acropolis, on the rocks in front of the Parthenon, and she woke up wondering if that had changed her, if there were a place in the world that would change you, just by being there. Maybe she'd end up somewhere like that. Now she looked for Adri back in the kitchen to see what was cooking.

I'm going up to Aswan next month, Adri. Just a short reporting assignment, a week or so. But before that I go to Kampala.—Adriana was opening a tin of anchovies and forking the oily contents onto a cutting board, separating each one with a tiny fork, laying them out side by side.—You ever been there?

Tess watched her, so at ease. As if she never threw her hands up and said: I'm 55 and alone and with nothing to show for it but a bunch of Egyptian knicknacks! But no, she didn't think like that, and so wasn't like that. She arranged the anchovies into orderly rows.

I was there once, Tess—together they carried the food to the table and everyone sat to eat—for a study of the Nile, its history and its future, the water hyacinths and changes in the medio-ambiente. I had to go all the way up to Lake Victoria for research. Oh, Uganda. It was many years ago I was there. Mmmmm, there was a singer who took me around in his big silver Mercedes. He was very sweet, but Dios mio, he was the worst singer in all of Uganda. We went to see a concert of young people, orphans. It was in the back of the orphanage, an event paid for by a rich actor. There was a teenage girl, completely bald, and she sang like her life depended on it. I couldn't help think that there was something stripped away between her and what she was singing, like she was singing straight to the sky. Beautiful. And then my singer got up and sang some ballads like, excuse me, like an American with all those false sentiments. Everyone went mad. They loved it. He was a big star, it appeared. I wanted to go back to my hotel, and of course he wanted to escort me to my room. Oh oh oh. I was so embarrassed.

Abim fiddled with his fork. Laura shoved pasta into her mouth. Delicioso, Adri.

My grandfather used to make this: Spaghetti al limón. Just a little lemon and parmigiano. I added the fish. I saw it somewhere in Italy. It's good, no? She held up a fork with an anchovy dangling from the tine, speared through its tiny gills.

The night came quickly and Adri got up to turn on the overhead lights, which shone through little glass beads onto the posters and the high white walls, the brown molding, the pale green ceiling, and over the varnished tabletop, the beads of oil in the glass bowl they served themselves from.

Tess sat back and set down her glass and saw Laura as she was then: wine-stained lips, the familiar strands of hair, that warm gray color that emanated from her, the darkened tone of her pale skin. Her shoulders straight and strong. A muscular woman. On her own like Adriana. Did she see her own future like that? Would she end up post-menopausal in a bohemian flat in some city where she would live forever as an outsider? Running from a silver Mercedes in Uganda. Was it disturbing? Magnetic? The delicate lines in Adri's face as she laughed, her papery skin, dotted with tiny moles. A fine, experienced leader, perhaps. At least for a time. Something raw between her and the sky. Tess felt her subjectivity begin to swirl with the wine at the bottom of the glass, rise up and intermingle with the beads of the chandelier above them. La Comunidad becoming unhinged and vagrant. These separations had happened many times and this wouldn't be the last time, either, Tess was sure. The night in Belgrade she'd told Katarina about Abim's new job in Cairo, their departure, Abim swinging his feet out over the river, like Carlos or Rafa in the air above the desert. Max flew back from Istanbul not suspecting that his family was about to be torn apart once again. It happens over and over. The only thing was to savor this moment, when they were together as true friends. You can count on her, on them, we'll stick with you, we'll keep in touch, this is all that matters, to our future, to our success, to our auspicious wanderings and flounderings. But it's true, even after these few months, this almost a year sitting here above Tahrir, or in Laura's flat in Garden City, hemmed in by the arcing crowd-control streets; Tess would miss her. It wouldn't be the same, now, out in the city where relationships went back generations, God knows, even centuries, or so it felt, swarming around in the streets that radiated away from Wust al-Balad. Here around this table it was just a thin web they clung to, or perhaps didn't. Just let it go. Giddy with separation. Further and further. The history of it, the thing that had taken their ancestors, Tess's and Abim's and Laura's and Adri's, across the Atlantic, mostly at times when it was unlikely they would ever return; they had sailed off into the unknown without looking back, without the possibility, to Argentina, to Mexico, to the USA. Like someone now heading way out into the solar system, and maybe, like the explorers of the past, expressing the worst thing about the culture they were fleeing from. So that was in them, all of them. The contagion they carried, knowingly or unknowingly. That discontent, optimism or cynicism, debt or capture or pure fright, however it may be, turned inside out. Adriana into the past of the Nile. Abim at the Delta or chasing Nasreddin and his brethren down the moulid alleys. Tess about to fly into orbit, letting chance take over, and Laura once again pushing ahead.

Laura as she was in Skopje on the balcony overlooking the Apaches, Laura as she was in Stella Bar surrounded by green glass bottles, or under Adriana's beaded chandelier, about to take the first job offer and set off to Istanbul, sending emails from the little apartment in Tarlabaşı while Tess was up the Nile. God, those weeks before her life on Mahmoud Bassiouny evaporated, when she still thought she would follow Abim, when she didn't know what she would do. To think Laura was already in the apartment in Tarlabaşı while Tess was pacing the halls in Gulu. The next thing was already happening and she didn't even know it. What a relief it would have been to know, but she couldn't. Still, Laura was already there, going to the office with Eren and Omar and everyone. Only years later to leave Tess alone, to come here, to do this, to become what she was now, heaving under the warmth of the hospital lights in St. Luke's, the purring and puttering of a baby's heart, another generation to continue that same discontent and relentless movement, from here to there to there.

Of Uganda Tess remembered nothing at all. Or almost nothing, like she'd smeared it out of her mind imperfectly. What remained most insistently from her few days in Kampala and assessing post-conflict conditions in the north was an incessant argument with herself about shame and complicity: what she was and what she could do, how deep was her skin color, what she could do to not do what she was doing, not be who she was being, but the argument was part of being that, so just stop. The first night she had been taken by her host to a large white-walled estate, a compound where the country director of a German organization was having a going-away party, or something like that. She could remember glasses and voices and white women in skirts and Ugandans in uniform and that alone was too much for her to bear. Trees off into the night. How could anyone stomach this situation? Adriana's teenage orphan girl singing her heart out to the sky. Maybe there was no way to see anything here. Like when she first arrived in Sarajevo and was walking down the steps from Gorica into the center, and realized that everything she saw, the lozenge-shaped holes in the walls of apartment buildings, the red wax-filled splatter holes in the pavement—*Sarajevo roses, the color of blood*—all of it only reflected her own delusions about the proximity of death and clarity. A grave insult to the Sarajevans, she told herself. The Kampala compound with its half-polite conversations and the drunken jokes of the IO workers. The only Bugandan word she learned that night was *mzungu*, which meant white person, and was not supposed to be an insult, so the IO workers said, laughing into their buffet cups. She could not remember herself, not what she wore, what she looked like, how awkwardly she refilled her cup. *Drinking mzungu.* She could see herself in the morning behind the apartment the job had rented for her: sitting in a plastic chair by a small swimming pool with monkeys in the trees above her. Even the monkeys provoked mixed feelings. *Monkey-watching mzungu.* Finally the driver appeared and he was silent and formal with her, so she stared out the window in silence. They passed a big white temple in the middle of Kampala that she only much later realized must have been Jain.

The work was up near Gulu, in the north of the country, where she spent several days with the driver whose name she forgot and an Italian HIV researcher whose name she also forgot, who she left at the table in the hotel in Gulu as she went off to bed. He sat talking to two women, round and robust and with colorful scarves around their heads. And even though he talked to them politely, the fact of the Italian laughing and the women laughing as they sat together in the otherwise empty restaurant led her down a trail of conclusions that made her shake her head—Enough—as she walked off to her room. She lay in the cool hotel sheets of Gulu and let it all fade into a blank grayer than Slovene clouds. What she might have ever thought about Mitteleuropa, about the Belgrade artists when they seemed both milquetoast and arrogant. What she was in Gulu.

Her head was full of conclusions drawn from the reading she'd done, about Nilotic people of the north and Bugandans in the south around Kampala, about hierarchical vs. stateless decentralized communities, about Idi Amin and Rwanda and Congo and the ravages of the LRA. When she walked the rows of tarp-covered refugee tents during the day, green and brown here instead of the white of the Balkans—even the refugee camps in Europe are white, she said to herself—the camp director, a straight-backed guy from Gulu, spoke to her rapidly and optimistically, led her through the facilities, laughed with people he stopped to speak to. Rows of tarp-covered frames, some filled with supplies, set with tables, and everywhere alleys, footpaths beaten in by the feet of children, children running and playing under the unremembered sky. The camp director spoke all the while and she looked at him from far within her eyes. She realized that in fact she was not here, that she did not see him and he did not see her, and that as long as what she finally wrote and turned in didn't interfere with the camp programming, with the chances for funding, with access to materials, her visit would be scrubbed from the memory of the place entirely. And that was her only chance of success.

The stoic driver and the camp director brought her from the camps to the villages in the surrounding area that were being resettled. Militias had come through and people took refuge in the camps, which were supposed to protect them. But now the fighting had mostly quieted, so people were beginning to return to their villages. Meaning to a spot between footpaths with access to fields, where they could rebuild their houses and return to the way they used to live. Tess in front of the round earthen house of a man showing off his fields: manioc and sweet potato and corn. Everything burst out of the ground. There was no problem at all. As soon as there is no more war.—The fighting stops, he said, and we come back to our houses, and it's like nothing ever happened.

On the way back to Kampala they were overtaken by an LRA caravan coming back from South Sudan where there had been peace talks, or some kind of meeting to reach an agreement. Whatever that meant. She had heard about the talks, of course, everyone had. The LRA caravan was on the front page of the papers. And now here they were. A series of ten or eleven black vehicles with armed escort. This militia associated with arms-wielding twelve-year-olds, who just the year before had shot two aid workers around here. The stoic driver stopped their car, pulled over, and became even more motionless as the caravan passed. But the torsos emerging from the open roofs of the vehicles were of grown men, their shoulders draped in ammunition and arms holding kalashnikovs, their eyes covered by dark glasses. Militants with their proud dark glasses. This is as far as I'll ever go, she thought. My eyes are too thick.

The caravan passed without incident, like Clinton's caravan when he drove through the streets of Tetovo in '99. Nothing happened then either.

The afternoon before she left she had been near Lake Victoria. Probably the Italian HIV specialist had driven her there but when she pictured herself she was alone. She stood not far from the lake and before the shore was a small tree, not much taller than she was, and next to the tree was a water buffalo, and in the shallows with one knee bent stood a heron or crane or some long-legged white bird. The water buffalo stood facing the bird and the lake, and from the thin trunk of the tree hung a suit jacket, as if someone had come by and removed their jacket and hung it from a nub on the tree like it was a coatrack. She looked around to see whose coat it could be, but there was no one in sight. She looked at the water buffalo, who looked at the bird, and then finally turned to look at her, the water buffalo, with the bird minding its own business, and the jacket hanging from the tree. This image inspired no reaction in her, a mild sense of laughter and lightness. She couldn't remember if the lake had been beautiful, what color it was, or why she had gone there at all. This I will carry with me, she'd told herself.

Back at the hotel in Kampala she sat next to the pool and watched the monkeys in the trees and read a novel someone had given her in

Cairo, a Mahfouz novel or maybe something else. *Reading mzungu.* No. She didn't remember that either. Much less the ride back to Entebbe and the 3 AM flight to Cairo and then to Aswan.

It was difficult to work with Mubarak, so the Brit development guy told her, but they managed. Predictable at least. The Brit was a scruffy, red-nosed fellow still working for DFID like he had in Prishtina. They met in Zamalek before she headed back to the airport to fly south to inspect a series of projects in the upper Nile, economic development in Nubia, communities affected by the Aswan dam.

Our man in Aswan's called Hamed. He's a novelist.—The Brit fished through his bag until he found a magazine clipping and handed it over.—That's him.

The clipping was from some francophone journal on the Middle East, an article called *Le Conscience D'Afrique*, with a picture of Hamed's face in shadow, a noble Semitic nose emerging in profile. He'd written several books about Upper Egypt, so it seemed, stories of village life.

Fine, Tess said, and two days after returning from Uganda she was squinting along the Aswan corniche, just off the plane, checking in to the Hotel Abu Simbel. There was no pool in back, and no monkeys, either; instead a garden hidden from the street by a row of acacias, circular tables for smoking and drinking.

Perhaps she would get used to it, this jetting around, consultant life. She'd always hated consultants, thought of them as imperious, ignorant. Now, she thought, maybe they, like her, had just been floundering, needing work, trying not to freeload off spouses or parents or girlfriends or whoever.

She slept fitfully and at noon from her seat in the hotel lobby saw a willowy, rust-colored man with a loping stride and a focused but gentle gaze coming for her: Hamed. He was polite and restrained and did not offer his hand for her to shake. Instead he led her to an old white car, folded himself in and drove further up the Nile. The city thinned until they were on a gently curving and beaten-up two-lane with palms separating them from the river. On both sides its banks gave way to mountains of rock and sand. They drove up behind a local combi, stuffed with men traveling from here to there. These men, on the way somewhere in the heat of the day, rocked impassively as the combi bounced over the potholed highway.

He parked by the side of the road in front of a dense village, and Tess had to hurry to keep up with his long and wiry legs as he strode through the alleys of houses made of compacted earth. He waved an arm over the surrounding fields that had been restored for village use. Now the local people could sift through the alleyways to their fields of cotton and wheat, to their collective gardens of tomato and spinach.

This is Sasida. It's built around a Fatimid tomb, a great sheikh lived here.

He led Tess up a rocky ledge to a mudbrick house overlooking the river.

My house.

As they walked in an elderly woman rose from a mat where she'd been sitting and kissed Hamed and raised a hand to Tess. The woman's eyes were covered in cataracts and her bony fingers reached forward. She took Tess by the elbow, walked her through the house and out back to a large tree with thick spiraling branches that rose up from the center of the garden overlooking the valley and river below.

Hamed followed them outside, signaling down to the land below them.

Nothing has changed here since ancient times. Pharaohs, Arabs…
Here all that matters is the relationship between man and the Nile.

He sat down at the base of the tree, his head against the trunk and arms outstretched and palms turned up toward the sheltering branches.

This is where I learned to read.

Pharaohs, ancient customs, it made no difference. Kansas or Egypt or Mexico City. We are all born in the navel of the world. You can stay right there and see everything there is. Now that Tess had been as far as she'd ever go, waiting for the LRA caravan to pass on the Kampala–Gulu road, she could see this, too, know it, in fact, as well as Hamed did. Though the fact that he'd always known it was an advantage, really, she had to admit.

They sat at a low table and ate dark red tomatoes and a viscous stew of cumin-laced molokheya. There was no wife to be seen, but a little girl ran out from the back, a dark and open face and lovely large eyes.

This is Nada, Hamed introduced her. And she walked over and lay her arm on Tess's shoulder.

Nada. Tess relished the beautiful name, which referred to the morning dew.

Nada tucked in next to her father and they sat and ate. Tess watched Hamed scoop the viscous stew into her mouth with flatbread that looked fresh and flavorful, not the chewy cardboard of central Cairo.

Hand some to our guest, Hamed said.

And Tess took a piece from her molokheya-covered fingers, savoring the taste and the moment of stillness with Hamed's family. His daughter, his mother. Where was his wife?

Hamed cleaned the girl's mouth with his hand and she ran off into the garden. They digested under the tree above the Nile, the sun high above the ancient valley.

Perhaps Hamed was a widower, Tess thought. Perhaps she could stay here and occupy the space left behind, remain in this navel of the world with the Conscience D'Afrique, raise little Nada with her dewdrop name, which in Serbian means hope and in Spanish means nothing.

After lunch Hamed led her to the tomb of the Fatimid sheikh, where he stood still but not solemn, head nodding at the monument, a stone construction that Tess would have guessed was a village well. But when Hamed turned away from the tomb he faced out over the river valley again.

This is the true Egypt. Not the Arabs in Cairo. What did Arabs ever do up in Upper Egypt? Lay in the sand, die of thirst. The only thing they left was their language.

Tess wondered what she could report to DFID in Cairo, what could she say about the fields of Sasida. As they started to descend from the tomb, a woman called to them from an open doorway, beckoning for them to enter. From the outside the house was made of pale gray mudbricks like the rest, but through the tiny arched passage they entered a space of multiple vaulted ceilings and doorways and stairs between rooms bare and open but somehow complicated. Everything was covered in some mixture of earth and stone and talc so that it looked like gray marshmallows had been melted over the whole thing. Not a single straight line to carve edges in the extreme Nubian sun. No furniture, not even a rug. Just a series of women, five or twenty or a hundred years old, in dark and iridescent gowns. Children played train in the center of the space, holding on to each other's waists, running around and around in circles. In the corner was a woman whose face was a vortex of wrinkles, huge silver halfmoons dangled from her ears. Eyes buried somewhere beneath layers of dried cheek.

A woman is in labor, Hamed explained. They're asking me to bring the midwife.

The pregnant woman was in the back, in one of the dark chambers, and Tess slowly heard noises coming from there, a low groan that increased in intensity, surrounded by the high-pitched chatter of the other women. Tess had never heard this sound before, the groans of a woman in labor. Hamed indicated that they must go, giving Tess as an excuse, but one of the women, middle-aged and straight-backed and authoritative, indicated they were to do no such thing. Hamed agreed to refill the water jugs, not at the tomb but in another alley behind the house where there was a spigot. Tess found herself carrying water, too, then sitting with the women, who inspected her clothes and her shoes and held her hand.

So big, were the only words Tess could understand. So big and pale.

I'll go bring the midwife, Hamed said. Can you wait for me here?

Someone from the family brought out a tray with tea and sugar and Tess sat on the clean white surface, so big and pale, drinking her tea. And occasionally she heard the woman's groans from the back, groans becoming growls and screams. Even though she knew what the noises were, Tess found them frightening. She felt her ears twitch and asked permission to walk through the village, stepped outside into the alleys and paced around the tomb of the sheikh.

Finally Hamed appeared, followed by a woman who ducked into the house and began to order people around. Tess stayed in the alley in the lengthening shadows until Hamed appeared and called to her. He told her they had to wait a bit longer, and then returned to the family. And Tess was alone in the alley, the village quiet except for the bustle of the family and the screams of the woman that rose up out of the house and surrounded her, burrowing into her brain, and only once did she try to see what was going on inside.

They called her in when it was over to view the gooey extraterrestrial that had been brought into the world, women gathering blood-soaked cloths into bundles. Tea and chatter and finally Hamed led her back to the car and drove to Aswan. She got out and leaned over to say goodbye to him, to thank him for the day. He smiled and thanked her, too, but didn't get out, and quickly pulled off. Tess watched the car disappear around the corner before she went inside.

Back behind the Hotel Abu Simbel she sat alone, surrounded by tables of men smoking and drinking from green bottles of Egyptian Stella like in Cairo. She sat still stunned by the labor pains and Hamed's beautiful daughter and the white curves of Sasida. She thought the sheikh had picked a wonderful place to die. She supposed that Hamed would die there, too, and that would be perfect for him. His mother would bury him, howling at his funeral, because his mother was sure never to die, not like his wife, or supposed wife, mother of Nada, of hope and of nothing. Tess wondered where Abim would die, where Laura and Adri would die, a stripe of green at the end of the world, a swimming pool behind an abandoned hotel. As for herself, she would rise above the world like smoke and circle and dissipate and be forgotten, never having lived, never having been born, and going nowhere.

The dark and enveloping sound was shattered when Dr. Shen flicked on the light switch and flooded the room with harsh white light. The nurse behind the doctor held out a pair of powdery latex gloves. The screams of Sasida receded, the unceremonial goodbye to Hamed, who she never spoke to again, not even calling to fact-check her report. He disappeared back to his tree and his tomb and Tess was there in the bright light with Dr. Shen, who slid the refracting ring off her finger and set it on the instrument tray. Tess watched as she patted down a spot on the mattress then took a seat. Her crossed legs pointed toward Laura's shoulder.

Could I have some gel?

She extended her left hand, and the nurse squeezed out a colorless substance, tiny bubbles caught inside it, from a packet he had ripped open.

Aaaaah, eeeennnnh.

The nurse turned toward Laura for a second as a contraction came on. Barish grunted and got up from his chair. Tess shook herself to attention and started to move toward her, too, her role now becoming automatic, Laura's need for her, but the doctor shot them both a glance that said stop. Tess pressed her back against the wall, and Barish dropped back into his seat.

Dr. Shen rocked Laura with her right hand and held her left hand in the air, two fingers out as if gingerly holding a cigarette. She sat propped on the bed as if it were a divan, a fainting couch, the glistening gel perched on her latex fingertips—So it'll be Joanne, then?—talking to the nurse about some hospital business—Well, they'll be glad to have her, I suppose—as Laura squeezed her eyes shut and suffered through the continuing tightening of her uterine walls, dilation, through the wild force of the galloping heart.

The contraction came to an end, the sound slowed again, and Laura's neck muscles released. An ionic charge had tightened the air, and as the internal pressure left Laura's body it loosened, and Tess could drift back down to earth.

The doctor twisted around so her shoulders squared with Laura's abdomen.—Now, I'm going to check how you're coming along.—and with her right hand she flipped up Laura's hospital gown so her thighs and belly and hairy vagina, flush with blood, were exposed to the bright white light of the room.

Bring the soles of your feet together, knees apart.

Laura did as she was told, forming a diamond shape with her legs. Dr. Shen placed her right hand on Laura's thigh, then lowered her left hand into position and inserted her fingers into Laura's vagina.

You're going to feel my hand, the doctor was saying. You're going to feel my fingers.

She paused as Laura's eyes popped open, surprised, then dropped back inward, concentrating on the feeling of the doctor's hand. Laura turned to face Tess, her eyes saying: What's happening? It was as if the doctor's whole hand were going to disappear into Laura's abdomen. A gush of wind from inside Laura's body could have blown her clear across the room.

Tess stepped around to the other side of the bed, with her back to the windows and Barish in the green plastic armchair, and picked up Laura's hand and held it. Laura gave her a squeeze.

The doctor spoke to Laura:

Now you're going to feel some pressure.

And with that Laura squeezed Tess's hand harder and harder until she would break it, so intense was the pressure coming from the elegant fingers of Dr. Shen, whose eyes narrowed in concentration. What was she doing in there? Laura pressed the back of her head against the mattress and squeezed Tess's hand.—Mmmmmh, mmmmmh.—She was trying to be good.

Laura squeezed and Tess felt a wave of sadness come over her. She had never been able to shake things off like Laura could. And now look at her, wincing and fretting. Labor pains, Tess thought. I will never do it. It will never happen to me. I will never love anyone enough to do it, will never let myself be taken over like that. I will just continue to be who I am, slowly and eventually and then it will cease to be relevant. In the air above Aswan or still in Istanbul or wherever. Back here watching the Hudson rise. I'll come see Laura's baby and play with it and buy it things, bring things from wherever I am and watch the storms through the windows. And that will be enough. I'll go back to my life, which is this, where I am right now. In this room right here with these people.

Tess on the flight back to Cairo, and again in the rattling cab along the raised section of the highway that wound past the old city toward downtown, stopped in traffic outside the second-story windows of the buildings there, the road back to the apartment on Mahmoud Bassiouny, to Abim. But when she walked in and dropped her bag on the floor, she heard not only Abim's voice in the other room but another as well. Her half-brother Max was sitting right there with Abim at the table, the rush of traffic out the window.

What? she said, confused.

Yes, Max answered, and got up to throw his arms around her.

When?

Just today, he said.

A year and a half since they left him in Belgrade, bereft on his sofa overlooking the city and the Danube in the distance, Max who thought they would never leave Belgrade, who had believed Tess when she said she thought of Belgrade as heaven.

As always Tess was aware of the ways they looked alike, despite their different mothers. Even though neither of them looked much like their game-footed, deceased father, he had bestowed on them the same downturned eyes and mops of brown hair.

Where have you been? How did you get here?

An overnight bus from Sinai, but mostly I've been in Syria.

A country nearby. Abim's country.

Now in their Cairo apartment Max told them of ending his

relationship with his scientist girlfriend in Belgrade, losing her to a job in an observatory in Cape Town. He talked of ending his contract with the organization they'd both worked for in Serbia, breaking his lease, his loneliness and confusion. Thoughtlessly he'd jumped on the Balkan Express to Istanbul, then slowly across Turkey, chancing upon a room at a Catholic rectory in Antioch, where he heard about a monastery in Syria, an hour from Damascus. Respite, it appeared to him. Syria as it was then. That's where he'd go.

You take a bus from Damascus, he said. And then a car drops you off at the base of the mountain. Then you climb winding stone switchbacks straight up the face of the cliff, something from an old kung fu movie.—He was impressed, she could see, just thinking about it.—Then at the top is the monastery, simple and made of stone, looking out over the valley, with arid peaks behind it. It was built in the fourth century but abandoned during the Crusades. It was empty until recently, when an Italian Jesuit had it reconsecrated. Now it's a working monastery. There are three novices and the father. Some Arab kids come up from the town nearby. They make cheese, they study. There are a couple of caves turned into cells to sleep in, and a small chapel for prayers.

Prayers?

Tess thought if only Laura were still in Cairo she could cure him. They'd met in Skopje in '99. Max had finished editing his montage of war footage in Sarajevo and arrived just as the generals signed their peace agreement, ending the war. Tess watched the camps she'd worked in all summer empty at alarming speed, grim and pessimistic. But Laura was high on adrenaline, getting ready to go in with the Marines.

I'm ready for anything, she said.

Laura and Max emptied several bottles of wine on the balcony of her house overlooking the kidney-shaped pool. There'd been a charge to their banter, Tess remembered. If only Laura could be here to smother his impatience with her warmth, he might have stayed. But she was gone already. Otherwise who knows, maybe it would have been Max instead of this špicoglav Turk. Then they really would have formed a family, like they were always about to do. Max wouldn't have gone back to wandering the barren hills in Syria, to disappear into another supposed holiness. His divinity washed away by the power of Laura's thighs, sweating and heaving on the hospital bed. Maybe then Tess, too, could have cured Abim.

At least Barish here has that going for him: he's worldly.

Instead Max told them of his life at the monastery. He washed and cooked and did chores around the household, but mostly he was free to do what he wanted, which was to be there among the barren mountains.—Up there it's possible to be really alone. I walk for hours. I sing to myself. It feels good to be up there.

He sat at the table and talked, asked Tess about Kampala and Gulu and Aswan. But really he was interested in Abim, in his explorations with Nasreddin.

They walked across the city, through Zamalek and to the Kit Kat waterfront. Tess learned that Safiya and the boys were in Alexandria, so she found herself on cushions inside the houseboat, listening to the talk of these three voyagers in the beyond. Nasreddin trying to explain what had attracted him to Islam:

It was the open space. Emptiness. The open spaces of the mosques became a metaphor for the clear unobstructed light cast by Islam over the world.

But there is so much about punishment, Max was saying. I mean, do you truly accept that there is such a thing as hell?

Max looked so sincere in his questioning, Tess thought. What was he missing?

There is nothing but one truth, Nasreddin said, so what is meant by hell is the mistaken sense of separateness. A delusion, but a deep and powerful one.—Tess tasted the word: *hell.* She considered it her home, naturally. Licked by flames.—The feeling of separateness is excruciating. To be damned is to walk through life suffering from a delusion of God's absence. Then to die and pass through the day of judgment.

What should be called the day of religious truth, Abim interjected. It's clarifying.

Exactly, said the pale-eyed Slovene. They pass through that moment and are thrown into the fire. And once they're there, they feel its permanence, they understand they were always headed toward this place, they were asking to be there, and their terror and confusion were simply doubts about fate, about the limits of their power. Maybe there was something they could do? They sought free will, liberation, but that in itself was a move against the one truth. Now, dwelling as they did in the fire, they could see it for what it was. The fire was the fire of purity, burning away their delusions, and when they see that, it becomes sweet.

Nasreddin sat up tall for once, concluding his lecture:

Once all doubt is removed, what was once felt as lacerations of flame transform. Instead they carry the sting of intimacy, a sensation so overwhelming that the poor souls had doubted it, misunderstood its sweetness as pain. So you see, what is called hell is really just an attitude toward life.

Tess walked behind Abim and Max as they stepped through Zamalek on the way home, continuing their talk, their investigation into these areas that made no sense to her, only made her despair. I was always on my way here, she thought, and I was always on my way to the flames. She had trouble seeing the sweetness in the situation, the sting of intimacy and the fire of purity. Rather than evaporating in the light of true religion, the distance and confusion she felt were solidifying, and she didn't know how to talk about it with anyone. Not with Max when they were alone at night after Abim had gone to sleep. She suspected there might be something so damaged within her, not even Abim's patience could drive it out. A contamination was taking her over, transforming her into something else. She watched Abim and Max walking side by side like two best friends. What should be her family. Abim already talking about the transfer to Lebanon he'd applied for.

We'd be close to you. When you've had enough of the monastery and want to come down to hang out and swim in the sea, you can stay with us in Beirut.

Tess tried to imagine it, herself starting out once again as a spouse, or continuing this flight from one consultancy to another, a sea of confused and useless actions. Her delusions, a deep and powerful sense of her own separateness. What haunted her was not the creeping knowledge of fate, but the yawning absence within her. Her sister and father and mother and brother. The years in the Balkans. Cairo. She tried to imagine a home she could go to. A life with Abim in Beirut. A little apartment in Hamra not far from the sea. But no light of clarity came over her. She was driven by something else, something she was unable to name or know. Elusive but irresistible, what had floated up and out of her when she sat behind the Hotel Abu Simbel. After the birth, she thought. Like here like now. Her nut of a uterus sending her messages.

Four, said the doctor to the nurse. Eighty. Minus two.

Tess stepped out of the way of the nurse as he moved to the workstation to record these numbers.

The doctor now turned to face Laura.

Things are progressing, she said. But slowly.

Which was impossible for Tess to understand. She took a seat in the green plastic armchair by the window, watching Laura's vacated face staring up at the ceiling.

Slowly?

We may have to do a slight intervention.

Laura lay with a hand on her belly, and when the light returned to her eyes it was white and beaming, focused.

What are you talking about?

The doctor now placed a hand just below Laura's.

The baby's head is here. It's relatively low, which is good.

Barish bent slightly forward as if he were trying to see what was in the doctor's hand.

Your contractions are coming along, but your dilation hasn't increased in the last few hours, and your water still hasn't broken. I'm just going to give you a little poke, to open the amniotic sac, and that will help get things moving. Okay?

She moved her hand to Laura's thigh, as Laura lay back on the bed, facing the ceiling. Barish stepped back to get out of the way of the nurse, who was holding out a long thin instrument wrapped in paper and plastic. Dr. Shen took it, setting it on the tray by the side of Laura's bed, while the nurse opened a cabinet behind the workstation and pulled out a green nylon package, unfolding it into a large square of cotton padding.

Up you go, he said, looping an arm through Laura's bent knees. He lifted her ass off the bed and slid the layer of padding underneath her, then set her back down.

Barish picked up the ice bucket, and came to Laura with a piece of ice in his hand, which he pressed against her forehead. The nurse grabbed a pink plastic bowl, dumped some water and ice into it, took a white hand towel and soaked it.

Here, he said, handing the towel to Barish. Wring it out and put it on her forehead.

Barish did as he was told, letting the water drip into the bowl and then laying the towel over Laura's tangled strands, water streaming down either side of her face, clenched against the pain.

The doctor and nurse waited for the contraction to pass. Barish leaned in and pressed the cloth against her forehead, like the nurse had shown him, until she batted it away like it was an invasion. Tess watched drops of ice water arc toward the window.

Breathe, Barish said to her. Just breathe.

She hiccupped and groaned again but finally did catch her breath, carefully with her mouth open, sucking air in and letting it go, making a whistling sound, and soon the tension passed from her face like a cloud. She grabbed Barish by the wrist and brought his hand to her chest.

Okay, said Dr. Shen.

Barish got up and moved out of the way and again the doctor took her place on the bed, perched with one leg crossed over the other. The nurse pulled a strip at one end of the sleeve, removing a long plastic rod with a little hook at the end, and handed it to the doctor.

The poker. Like a fire poker or a knitting needle.

Tess imagined what was to come, that thing sliding into Laura's body, through the cervix and into the uterus, where the baby was enclosed in a skein of flesh, a thin layer constructed by Laura's body, somehow, to enclose the baby, where the baby had lived now for nine months, swimming in the juices of Laura's body, feeding, absorbing, releasing, building. The poker about to enter and break the surface, release that tension.

When the screams echoed over the walls of the house in Sasida, Tess had approached and peered into the courtyard. Across the open spaces, still white even in the darkness, she saw the form of the woman in the small room. She was standing up, with her knees bent, pressing against the wall of the house, undulating, moving her hips forward and backward as if she were fucking. She let out a scream and Tess thought she saw the head of the baby coming out of her, appearing there upside down as the woman moved her hips forward and back, forward and back, the baby's head just a wad of goo with eyes and hair. Tess was not sure but it seemed to her that the baby's eyes were open, staring in her direction. She turned away so as not to see more.

And now Laura. Dr. Shen with her long delicate fingers. And the strange nurse. She realized she didn't even know his name. And Barish still holding Laura's hand, his salt and pepper hair.

Okay, now you're going to feel some pressure again, and then you'll feel some leaking of fluids. There may be blood, as well, from the cervical opening.

Laura lay back and closed her eyes and nodded.

Dr. Shen slid the poking instrument into Laura's body, and Laura remained still with her eyes shut, clenched up as if expecting it to be painful.

There, Dr. Shen said. Very good.

And Laura opened her eyes. What had happened?

Tess saw a growing puddle of fluid on the cotton pads that Laura now lay on, an expanding circle of clear fluid.

Was that it? Laura said. Is it over?

That part is over, the doctor said. The fluid is clear. No meconium. That's very good.

And she smoothed Laura's hair with one hand, while with the other Dr. Shen handed the poking instrument to the nurse, who inserted it into a biohazard bag. Tess pictured a pile of used medical instruments somewhere, dripping with the clear fluid of birth sacs that had been poked, draining down into the ground.

Tess watched Dr. Shen pick up the diamond ring off the instrument tray and slide it back on her finger. There was a seriousness to her, Tess thought. She could trust her. She was a good person, a caring, patient person. Whoever had given her that ring could be happy. Next year maybe it would be her lying back and moaning, with someone else's hand on her thigh, talking about dilation as she screamed in pain. Or she would just blissfully slide out a perfect pale little pod of a baby into someone's arms and a white halo would shine around the perfect thing. And what about this one now? Laura's tangled hair and the pointy head of Barish joined in DNA interweave. What could it be like? A spirit from somewhere else, with its own destiny. Who would grow up to argue and rebel against these two, drive them crazy. Where would they even be? Somewhere up on high ground after the rise of the oceans and rivers, taking refuge on the upper floors of the building in Hell's Kitchen, the Hudson seething below. Barish AWOL somewhere and Laura breathing out her last breath in the bedroom. What boxes of photos would the kid show Laura? Digging through dead email accounts, image archives, to find scenes from Cairo or Istanbul, from Congo or Kosovo or New York as it was at another time, a time that seemed so ordinary and frustrating to us, but to the kid will seem nostalgic, magical. That was when things were happening! And what were my stupid parents doing?

I'm going off duty, the nurse said, pulling the latex gloves off his hands and depositing them in another receptacle for waste. But Joanne will be coming on. She'll take good care of you.

Barish reached over and shook the nurse's hand. Tess just nodded and then he was gone, his carotene scalp a flash in the icy light of the hallway, his polka-dotted socks around the corner. And behind him Dr. Shen disappeared, too, and the room felt empty. Tess went to turn the light off behind the closed door and the room fell into galloping darkness, lit only by the monitors: 90, 98, 102, 99.

Tess still in Cairo while Abim's days there were numbered. A last month of her hand in his hair, her not speaking her doubts, before his transfer came through and he was off to Beirut. Tess stayed to finish her contract with the Brit, to file her reports and look for work. Just a month and I'll be there, she'd said, but then when he was gone the apartment felt so big and spacious, and she wondered if she would follow, after all, if she wanted to be a spouse again, in Beirut or anywhere for that matter. Now she was alone and quiet and she felt happier than she'd been in years, for no reason, and that was the best kind of happiness there was, to be light and expanded for no reason like that. Abim and Laura were gone and even her brother was gone and she was alone. The cabs honked at her as she walked out of the Stella Bar. Yousry and Rasha took her to Sinai for a week and she jumped into the shallow water and it made no difference whether she was inhaling the beryllium and exhaust of Wust al-Balad or the clean fumes of the Red Sea.

When she talked to Max she futilely tried to explain this happiness—But you were always free like that—him calling in from Damascus and her in Egypt—and if you're here then we'll be close by again, like we were in Serbia.

Family, he said.

It had meant so much to him. Always. Since they'd met after the reading of their father's will, him thirteen and her eleven and her older sister Helen sixteen. They were from the city and he was from the suburbs, and Helen had tried to civilize him, to initiate him into their world. He'd practically moved in with them, into their paintchip house behind the art museum. Helen treated him like he was soft and ill-equipped, but Tess had loved him, imitated him, wanted to be a boy, too.

Later they scattered. Helen to San Francisco and Max to New York. That horrible phone call when they'd found out about Helen's drug-induced seizure, flown out for her funeral, that shock that had gone on for months, that had never really stopped. Tess alone in Kansas City, half-assedly in the local university, hitchhiking through the plains and prairies, looking for something in that emptiness. Until she'd found H2O's work program in Bosnia, and Max to escape his Attorney St haze had joined her, then picked her up in Skopje after the embezzlement washout and taken her to Greece where they'd sat on the shaking acropolis. By the time Max was installed in Belgrade their visits had been routine.

Now was a chance to have it again. She could hear the plea in his voice.

But to her it wasn't like that. No job, no reason. She couldn't go through that again. But maybe it wasn't work that she wanted, even. That wasn't the problem. It was that she felt pulled by the giddiness of solitude. Not to bond or form a partnership. Not to set up in a little apartment where Abim could sip tea at the table. She thought of Laura. Thought of Adriana, too, even though they were seeing less of each other. She thought of her mother about to retire, of her sister's ashes swirling off the Golden Gate Bridge. All the women alone, and she felt satisfied with what she was, certain of something for once.

Everything I've done, she thought, was just for this feeling. This certainty that despite everything she was whole. The lousy flatbread from the corner tasted delicious, the lemonades at the teashop, the insipid smoke of the shisha. Tess woke up every morning in the traffic rush and felt the space of herself alone. Some point of maturation, she wondered, finally.

She sat in Horreya, drove in cars with Yousry and Rasha, ceased to make any pretense of looking for work in Beirut. But lied to Abim that she was.—Yes, she said. I sent it.—Him talking of contacts at organizations, the diplomatic corps. Cairo now weightless. The whole region. The stink of white phosphorous in Iraq. The thought of trails of refugees, networks of small arms, the sores on the cheeks of the children in Gulu, the coathung tree along Lake Victoria.

She called Laura in Istanbul and talked to her and Laura did understand.

I know, she laughed. They get old, don't they.

That's not what I mean, Tess thought, but didn't say anything.

Laura said she could get her a job in Istanbul if she wanted. Would see if she could squeeze another salary out of the budget. Come and be colleagues. Rather than sit in job searches in Beirut or these useless consultancies. The whole world is here, she told Tess.

Look at her now, undulating like that, the muscles of her uterus. Laura. But then even though it didn't mean the same thing to her, she understood something about Tess's solitude. And that was enough.

When Tess finally opened up Abim's face on the computer screen, prepared to tell him she wasn't coming, she could see the different quality of his being now that he was in Beirut. Abim had always been on his way to Lebanon, she thought. Which he would agree with. She could see, in the bright light and pixelation, flecks of gray among his thick black curls. Maybe they had always been there, but no. It was only now. Now that he had finally made it to Beirut, to where he was always going, something had come unclenched and allowed the gray to express itself. A sign of satisfaction, of maturation like the open space Tess savored in the apartment on Mahmoud Bassiouny. But when she did finally tell him—I took a job in Istanbul, she said. I'm going there—and stomached his stunned acceptance, it didn't mean for her that she had got where she was going, only that she was finally somewhere, which was alone.—Will you try to come here eventually? he asked.—I don't know, she said—which was good, too, not to know, was enough for her, for now, maybe. Laura was there and Laura was also alone, and Tess felt that Laura had always been alone. When Tess had wandered across the US after her sister's funeral, slept with truckers and vagrants and whoever she came across, she had not been alone. She'd been doing it all for someone else, even if she didn't know it. But Laura, already in Skopje, had always been whole unto herself, and even this wouldn't change that, Tess thought. Not the hands of Barish on her belly, not even the child that was coming, driving Laura to squirm on the bed, with Barish rubbing her back, her face to the window, toward Tess in the green plastic-covered armchair, looking at her, then squeezing her eyes shut in pain, the intimate lacerations of that particular pain.

Tess spent her last days in Cairo back in the Green Valley, was there until the airport car service picked her up and she loaded her bag into the backseat. She was still shaken and uncomfortable, but once the car set in motion she relaxed, watching the chaos of the city out the windows. A traffic jam as they escaped downtown, but eventually driving on the upper level of the highway. She fell into the increasingly familiar trance of this motion, the road arcing gently, the car stopping when traffic held it up just outside the windows of these ancient houses, all the same tones of brown and tan and beige and gray, everything in the epic hiss of African sunlight, the bright haze of pollution, all the ingredients of the new millennium. She swerved in her thoughts behind the driver, who was listening to a cassette of

Qur'anic recitations, the slur of the aging cassette heightening the power of the sound as it penetrated Tess's brain.

Then the thump of the exit visa on her passport, finding her seat on the plane, looking out the window at the sunblasted tarmac. Where and who she was disintegrating into some other worlds of ignorance, freed from good intentions or expectation, from expectations of familiarity or consistency, just enjoying the ride. She felt a huge expansion within herself, as if she had finally committed to something.

She could feel a lead ball against her chest, hanging between her breasts, in a place scooped out of her sternum, and in it were all the things that had happened to her. She could feel it rotate against her skin and feel what was inside it, not just the things themselves, but their density, their nutritional value and toxicity. Somewhere in there was Tess and her sister in the back of the public library when they were children, was her climbing into the cab of a semi in Illinois, at a midnight checkpoint between Bihać and Banja Luka, swimming in the Adriatic, swimming in the Mediterranean, in the Red Sea, now laying back once the forward momentum built. Toward Laura, toward Istanbul. Going somewhere, God knows. Rising and falling.

Tess, Laura called. Where are you?

I'm here, she said, and leaned closer, then stood up, put a hand on Laura's hip and her back and pressed on her as she'd seen the nurse do.

Aaaaah, yes. Laura said. Do that, do that. More.

And Tess pressed down on her hip as Laura winced and screamed and made new sounds Tess hadn't heard before, that emerged from low in her throat and didn't sound human at all. Tess pressed and Laura writhed and convulsed slightly, unable to control herself, or unconcerned, moving her shoulders and chest as if she were trying to get comfortable, or to shake out of her own body.

I have to get up.

Laura started to heave herself from her side to her back and tried to lower a leg to the floor, her hospital gown caught beneath her.

Wait, Barish said.

He went around quickly to grab her, and Tess took her other shoulder as she managed to plant both feet on the ground.

Aaaaah! Laura winced. What's happening?

Fluid was dripping down Laura's legs and onto the floor. Tess reached to grab a paper towel and threw it on the tiles.

Watch out, it's wet.

Is it blood? Laura looked down, trying to see in the reddened darkness.

No, Tess said. It's clear. It's the same stuff. It's your water, I guess.

Laura stood in place, her hair smeared across her forehead, Barish holding her up by one shoulder, and looked as if she were about to do something, or say something, or go somewhere. Fluid still dripped from her, and the paper towel sopped in a puddle of it on the tile floor between her legs.

What do you want? Tess asked.

Let me just stand here for a second.

Tess watched her breathing heavily. Laura had both hands on the mattress, and she started to move her hips, rocking back and forth like the woman in Sasida. Barish held her, and Tess grabbed her other shoulder, and they looked at each other for a second, eye to eye, Barish and Tess.

You've got her? Barish asked.

Tess raised her elbows to acknowledge the obvious. Laura had her eyes shut and was just moving her hips, moving her swollen belly this way and that.

I've got you, Barish said, but Laura wasn't listening.

Ahhhhh, she said. Ahaaaah. My hips, my hips. It's like it's going to break open.

Tess began to squeeze her hips from both sides. Her skinny arms working as hard as they could. Barish held her from the side, and Laura pressed her ass back against Tess, who struggled to keep her footing.

Yes, Laura said. Do that.

Tess pressed as hard as she could.

Yes, aaaaaah, aaaaaah. Laura said.

Tess was mashed up behind her, her cheek against Laura's back. Barish in front of her somehow, his hands in her armpits. Laura clutched at his wrist with one hand, the other pressed against the mattress. The sound of the baby's heart rushed through the room, and some sweet and sour smell emerged from the mixture of sweat and fluid and the plastic of the monitors that hung above their heads.

Tess heard Barish laugh somewhere as she squatted down to try to get a better grip on Laura's hips. She heard the laughter and lost her grip.

I'm sorry, he said, but he still couldn't stop himself.

Laura leaned over the bed, breathless. The contraction had passed. Oh my god, she said. Oh my god.

I'm sorry, Barish said, still laughing.

Tess was still bent over behind Laura's ass, then she stood up and looked around. Her own system was flushed with adrenaline now. She looked at Barish and saw the slight freckles in his complexion. She would take him by the ears and squeeze his head like she'd squeezed Laura's hips.

Fuck, Tess said. You have to try that. And she started to laugh, too. Her face was taken over by the raw awkwardness of her laughter, which she could never control.

Laura gave her a hazy look of affection and crawled back up on the mattress—Oh my god—made her way onto her back and lay down, her chest still heaving.

Tess had a flash of Barish and Laura together, their bodies and faces together. She looked at him, smiling as he stopped laughing, his mouth hanging open slightly. Špicoglav Turk, she thought. But no, he wasn't bad.

Next time, you try, she said.

Barish nodded, still smiling.

Tess went over to the green plastic chair by the window and collapsed, her hips heavy and awkward and her arms burning. Barish stood next to the hospital bed, dunked the towel into the bucket of water and squeezed it on Laura's face. Laura turned to look at Tess, her eyes wild, her face wet with ice water.

You have to keep doing that, she said. Promise me.

Tess took the Havaş bus from Ataturk airport, huge boats in the Marmara out the window. She spotted Laura as they pulled up to Taksim, standing with her feet slightly apart, looking planted there on the sidewalk in front of a strip of fast-food joints. Tess was overwhelmed at first, but when she began to roll her suitcase down Istiklal, through the endless flow of crowds, shouting and strolling past piles of profiteroles and brand new movie theaters and flashing lights for clothes and dripping desserts, her heart jumped with the wide-open feeling of promise and possibility. The sense of arrival all over again. But this time it was different, she told herself. Alone, older, and decided. And when they got to Laura's little apartment in Aynalı Çesme and found out the floor downstairs was emptying and she could move in next week, it was meant to be. When you finally truly commit, things can't help but fall into place.

The next morning Laura led Tess down the very steep hill to the narrow building that was the offices of People in Flight. It was on a little cobblestone street that ramped down to the waterfront boulevard. These houses would have been home, Laura said, to the disappeared Greeks or Jews or Armenians. These days the neighborhood was full of Kurds and Turks displaced from the ravaged southeast, and there were still a few Romani families who had come in earlier. Westerners were moving in, threatening to displace everyone. But now laundry lines crisscrossed the alley, women weighed their elbows on windowsills, a man in a blue worker's jacket struggled to push his cart of biscuits around a truck loaded with watermelons. Off the crumbling façades bounced the amplified voices of men calling what's for sale through a mounted bullhorn. *Five lira five lira five liraaaaaa!*

They ducked into the doorway of the tiny building, a maze of useless dark hallways and oddly placed toilets, bedrooms used as offices, several kitchens, and a narrow staircase that led up to a rooftop set with potted plants where people could smoke cigarettes and wait and look at the Bosporus and the Old City and the Marmara in the distance. Container ships, ferries and fishing boats filled the strait and evil seagulls cawed relentlessly overhead.

The job was to assist asylum seekers, the lost and displaced who were stuck in the legal limbo of modern Turkey. They came from Afghanistan and Iran, but also East Africa, Congo, anywhere. She would work out of an office and those in need would wait in the hall to be called in one by one.

The whole world is here, Laura told her.

What was required was familiarity with immigration and asylum policies in the West, with criteria used by the UNHCR, and the patience to deal with hopeless situations.

People in Flight. Laura led Tess to a wide table at the end of the roof where a bald Turk sat behind a cup of coffee, looking into a laptop covered in stickers.

Eren will explain the work.

Eren was long and lean and gawky, with a quick and clear English acquired in London, so it sounded. His elbows pointed inward and his sleeves were pushed up his forearms exposing knobby, secessionist wrists. He stopped typing, grabbed a cigarette and took a sip from his steaming cup of coffee. He peered at Laura over horn-rimmed glasses that sat midway down the waxy ridge of his nose, as if to verify that she was serious, then started in with a laugh and a smile:

To the east Turkey has borders with Iran and Iraq and Syria, Georgia and Armenia and the little breakaway republic of Nakshevan, which is actually part of Azerbaijan. On the other side we have Greece and Bulgaria, the European Union. And on all sides the sea.—He stretched out an arm to indicate the container ships chugging up toward Russia.—The Aegean and the Marmara and the straits, but also the Black Sea to the north and a length of Mediterranean to the south that is truly wild.

Laura watched Eren with apparent pleasure. Tess turned to look at her, who looked at Eren, who looked back at Tess. A sip of coffee, the cry of seagulls, and he went on:

The rugged mountains to the east are basically impossible to navigate and control, and anyway Iranians can come across without a visa. So if you are Baha'i or gay or Christian you have *every reason to apply for asylum.*

Eren raised his thick eyebrows to indicate he was now coming to the good part:

Little did you know, Turkey has a strange law on the books, and the only people who can apply for asylum in Turkey are the ones fleeing persecution *in Europe.*—He pronounced the place-name through a stifled chuckle.—The law dates back to that delightful period known as *the rise of nationalism,* when the Ottomans lost their grip and Turks were run out of Bulgaria and Romania and the other territories in the Balkans. Although it's been nearly a hundred years, the law was never changed, and now that poor and hungry migrants are appearing from the Middle East and Africa, no one wants to rewrite the laws to accommodate them.

He paused, directing his languid almond eyes at Tess, to see if she was following.

This means that thousands of asylum seekers have no status at all.

Nowhere to go and nowhere to go back to. International law forbids Turkey from sending them back to their home country as long as there is reasonable expectation of persecution. But it will not allow them to apply for asylum, to immigrate and become part of the country. They are registered with the UN and entered into a long screening process, several meetings and examinations, the full weight of the world's most enormous international bureaucracy. The process takes years. Sometimes ten years. And through all that time they are not allowed to work, have no right to medical care, schooling, shelter. They are forced to live in the margins, beyond the margins. Their very existence is *extralegal*.

So what do we do? Tess asked.

What we do is very limited. We study policy and make recommendations, but the focus of our work is to provide legal assistance. We used to provide assistance to anyone who came to us.— He bugged out his eyes to express the insanity of such a situation.—We helped them complete paperwork, prepped them for interviews, made sure they understood the process. But there are tens of thousands of people in the country that need help, and look at us.—He waved his hand to indicate the poverty of their surroundings.—Now we only work with people who have already been rejected by the UN. If you can get through on your own, you're on your way. If you can't, and you need help, you come to us.

He paused to light one more cigarette.

Come to us, Tess thought, looking down at Laura's birthing body.

How could Laura do this to her? Now she would be a mom and she would take care of this baby and would never leave the US, would stay here and be full of love and inspired to be productive to take care of the kid, watch it grow and learn and deepen while Tess would remain alone, her own uterus a shrunken and shining nut of negativity, refusal, solitude.

She sat at the bedside watching Laura with her head back, her mouth open, breathing quietly, a gentle sound from her mouth to compete with the amplified sounds within her. As if she'd been turned inside out. And maybe that's what the baby was, what she was, too, a way of turning what came before inside out. Tiny misunderstandings or illuminations of what came before, through our ignorant and confused parents and ancestors and neighbors and teachers, brought to light. *Dando luz*, as Abim or Adri or the carotene nurse would have called it. Giving light to what's within. Some parts of Laura that were there when she was in the Balkans harassing municipal authorities, that accompanied her through the smuggling routes in the Western desert, in Sudan and Libya. What was once within now made visible. We carry our ancestors within us, Tess thought. But not in the sense that we are formed and led and limited by them. Rather we see and do what they never could, and in that way give them new life. So Laura's child will be a window into existence, gathering intelligence for her, expanding her world into new times and places and colors and people. And in that way Tess really was making of herself an endpoint, a refusal to give anything to her mother and father and the grandparents she hardly knew. Let their windows fall shut and go dark. Tess was the last glimpse into the world for whatever that line had been, whatever it had connected, evaporating with the shisha smoke above the Hotel Abu Simbel, or high above the streets of Hell's Kitchen, and that was enough. Let it end, she thought, and let them be satisfied with that, let them know what they have become. Perhaps that's why she had to seek out these lost causes, to impale herself on them, to feel best when things were at their worst. Even the joy of being alone and unmoored. It was a message to all who had come before her, given rise to her. She would take their delicate hearts, their asphyxiating throats and dead eyes and drag them all into the refugee camps of the future, show them to the philosophers of extinction, so that they could be satisfied with the outcome. Hmmph. Indeed. Enough. And then she could bury herself knowing that she had done what was best. She had done her part. There would be no celebrations and birthdays and cutesy ways of speaking, no noticing of a trait—your grandfather's ears or nose or laugh or way of coughing. There would be no quiet and loving observations, discovering things anew, no first days of school and puberty and sending them off into the world and hearing from them, getting calls in the night, meeting lovers and worrying and wondering. None of that. She would be who she was and she would end. She would scatter like her sister's ashes high above the bay, which is what she was doing anyway, had been doing all along.

I want to stand up again, Laura said. I think it was easier.

Barish steadied her as she threw her legs over the side, hardly had a moment to catch her breath between contractions. Tess would let Barish handle this one, she'd been at it all day already. It was his baby for god's sake.

Tess, she's still leaking, Barish said. Can you help me?

Reluctantly Tess got to her feet and for a moment she felt very tall. She sidled around the edge of the bed. The tiles were still streaked with fluid. The paper towels she'd thrown down weren't enough to absorb it.

Where did they get that pad from? Tess said.

I think it was in that cabinet, Barish motioned with his head to an upright cabinet against the far wall, still trying to support Laura as she got to her feet.

I need to stand up, Laura said as if to herself or the floor.

Tess opened the cabinet and it was full of piles of gauze and plastic jars and pouches of equipment. And there to the left were green squares of some nylon material, what she thought were the pads, so she opened one up, unfolded it and saw that it was what she'd been looking for. She kicked the paper towels out of the way, into a wad under the outlet against the wall, and unfolded the pad completely and put the green side down on the floor.

Great, Barish said, steadying Laura as she stood upright and started to moaning again, leaning back against him. Droplets of fluid fell on the cottony top of the pad.

I need Tess, Laura said. Tess, my hips. Please.

I can do it, Barish said.

No, Laura said. Tess, please.

And Tess, standing with another pad in her hand, about to replace the one sopping on the bed, now dropped it thoughtlessly and moved to help.

Please, Laura said. Ooooh.

Barish moved around to the side again and Tess squatted behind her and pressed her hands against her hipbones, as if trying to crush her pelvic bone.

Yes, Laura said, almost ecstatically. Aaaah.

Then the pain got worse and she made the same sound from deep inside her, some animal sound—Uauaawaaaahrrrggh—and Tess held on for dear life as the contraction moved through her. She could see her fingers clench up as she clawed at the top of the mattress.—Wwaaaahhhhhnnnngggnh.

When it was over Tess fell onto the floor on her ass, Barish still holding Laura under her armpits.

Oh my god, Laura kept saying. Oh my god.

Tess sat on the floor near the workstation where the carotene nurse had sat checking feeds and data from the monitors, the sound of the heartbeat returning to normal. Tess panted, exhausted. Behind her came a burst of light as the door was pulled open and then the overhead light switched on and they were frozen in that harsh cold light again, Tess looked up at Laura's ass as Barish tried to get her back onto the bed.

Hello-o, came a woman's voice from the doorway.

Why do they have to sing like that? Tess thought, turning around to see a frowsy cinnamon-haired woman in her sixties, red plastic glasses on her nose.

I'm Joanne, the woman said. I'm replacing Eduardo for the

graveyard shift.

Laura had climbed on top of the hospital bed and was on all fours, trying awkwardly to turn around, and Barish stood next to her not knowing what to do. Joanne clomped right in and sat down on the rolling chair behind Tess.

Tess got to her feet and said hello to the nurse, having managed to catch her breath.

Are you the immediate family? Joanne asked.

Well, I'm the father, said Barish.

Tess said nothing. Nurse Joanne peered at him over her glasses.

And what's your name?

Barish said his name, spelled it for her, and she pushed the chair over to the computer console and began typing.

And you are? She turned to Tess.

I'm just a friend, Tess said.

Now I have to ask a few questions, the nurse said. And she began to repeat the questions the first nurse had asked when she'd been admitted: Medication? History of illness? Operations?

I think she's already been through this, Tess said. When she was first admitted.

I know, dear, but I have to have the records myself, every time a new nurse comes on.

Laura heaved herself onto her side and lay panting on the bed.

Here, the nurse picked up the ice bucket and handed it to Barish. Perhaps you could fill this with some new ice.

I can do it, Tess said, reaching for the bucket, but the nurse cut her off.

I think it's better if the father does it.

And Barish grabbed the bucket and headed out to the hallway. When the door closed behind him the nurse turned to Laura.

Are you married?

What? Laura didn't understand.

Are you and the father married?

No, Laura said.

But you're in a relationship?

I guess, Laura said, still breathing with some difficulty.

Any history of domestic violence?

With him? Laura said in disbelief.

Mmmm hmmm, the nurse said, still typing in Laura's answers.

No. Nothing like that.

Very well, said the nurse, satisfied. She sat back, clicked a few tabs and called up Laura's statistics.

Very good, she said. I see you're past four centimeters. That's very good.

Tess now picked the pad she had dropped up off the floor and reached over to change the pad that was still soaking up fluid under Laura's body.

Could you help me? Tess asked the nurse.

Just a second, hon. The nurse looked through her reading glasses at the screen, then stood up.—Oh, I see, she said. And walked over to see where Tess was changing the pad. One second.—She reached over and grabbed a pair of latex gloves and snapped them on. Then, as Tess helped Laura raise her hips, she ripped the used pad off the mattress and slid a new one in place with the speed of a magician, it seemed to Tess.

I'll be back to check on you in a bit, she said. You're doing great. And she headed toward the door, meeting Barish on his way back in with a new bucket of ice.

Tess sat at her new desk in the PiF office, one hand clutching a mug of coffee from the pitcher-shaped thermos, opened her email, began to go through correspondence and documents and invitations and rejections. Laura in the next room conversed with donors, wrote up budgets, talked medium- and long-term strategy with Eren, while Tess, once she got a handle on the procedures, sat with clients and translators day-in day-out, looked at them, smelled them, listened to their stories, explained policy, tried to figure out what was possible, what anyone was expecting, and just pushed through the process, little by little. Mostly men, mostly alone, impassive, exhausted, haunted by the dire absurdity of the situation. Can't go can't stay. Can't work can't steal.

They said they were bringing us to Europe. We came here. The police said Turkey. No selling on sidewalk. Infractions delay process. Six months in the collective center. Eighteenth birthday coming soon. Get to Europe, to America, send for my family. Haven't heard, haven't seen. Just this 150 euros I need for the paperwork. The priest said I could help in the church. Maybe I stay there. Go back to the town, go back home. Engineer, construction, nurse.

Like the refugee camps in Macedonia and Gulu, the migrants to Tess were a vision of the future. This is how we live. In the world forming around them, movement itself was suspicious. For ordinary people, without elite educations and international connections, movement was to be kept to a minimum. Why do they need to move? Who will accommodate them? The impetus to go elsewhere was to be quantified and analyzed but not encouraged. As the diplomats and consultants and assessors and researchers traveled everywhere, more and more placeless, at home awaiting transport, in the nowhere spaces of stations and departures halls and mostly in screens and earpieces, the rest of the planet was penned in behind arbitrary borders, assigned satellite cities to live in, forbidden to move.

And if they tried to move, they would be found afloat on a boat between Bademli and Lesbos, or on the River Evro between Eastern and Western Thrace, shoved back and forth by various border enforcers until the planks of their vessel cracked and gave and they were engulfed by the rising waters.

The Somali interpreter was the large and loping, sad-eyed Omar. He bent himself up into the seat at the edge of the office and explained to Tess the UN's justification for rejecting the applicant who sat facing her. Omar with his thinning hair and sloping eyebrows, looked at the applicant, a teenage boy, with the concern of an older relative. He turned his head as they spoke, screwed up his mouth. Tess strained to understand more than a word or two from the Arabic she had learned in Cairo. The young man took his papers and went out, bent his head toward Tess two or three times and shook Omar's hand, briefly placing his palm against his chest.

If I had known, Omar said, I would never have left. I would have stayed in Mogadishu, or gone to Nairobi. Not here. At home at least I can beg a piece of bread from someone. But here they are afraid of Africans.

Omar had been in Istanbul five years, working for PiF the last three. His gentleman's ears inflamed with mercy, he sat long-limbed, one knee folded over the other, in a chair that looked miniature, fit for a schoolchild, his eyes bloodshot, his hands motionless.

He got up and loped up out of the room, heading for the roof to smoke another cigarette, squinting at the boats moving here and there, connected to the rest of the world in a way forbidden to him. Tess followed him so they could compare impressions of the interview. Was the boy telling the truth? Was he under eighteen?

We have always been taught about a superior being, a creator or a guiding power.—Tess stood with Omar as he smoked, remembering the fire of purity Nasreddin had described back on the Nile.—I start to think it might be not a superior but inferior being who is ruling us, Omar said. Look at us. Human being, we are heroic. We struggle. We are foolish but sometimes courageous. But may I be forgiven for thinking that this is ruled by a being with a mind like the police and lawyers, nothing superior to us. It is for us to be smart, to find joy, not to give up.

The boats went north and the birds flew south and Omar finished his cigarette and stubbed it out, headed back downstairs to interpret another case.

They sat and listened and advised.

Tess saw molecules and cell walls, Brownian motion, battering dots against barriers. She sat and listened, she wrote and she explained. She wondered at her own trajectory, thrown from bed to bed, unsettled and searching, and thought how in a way she might be happier if she were forced to remain somewhere, if her blue passport were confiscated and she could no longer pursue her idea of home, of finding a home rather than making a home, or being a home, which was all that was left to her now that she'd refused Abim's teatable in Beirut. She should be chained somewhere, she thought. Here, anywhere. Just here, where she was.

Don't be stupid.

At the end of the day she stepped back out onto the steep slope of the street that led up to Istiklal, and there she stood as the teeming crowds headed right and left, this manic strolling, shopping, eating, gawking. She sat on the corner squeezing lemon into a bowl of lentil soup, shaking hot pepper and stirring it with a spoon. She ripped off a chunk of lepinje, the same waxy bread as in Serbia, and dunked it into the soup. She relished the thought of being back on the Balkan peninsula, this chunk of land that spanned from Zagreb to the Bosporus. Now she had crossed its entirety. She was a person Balkanized, not in the sense of being divided up into imaginary countries, rather one of those who, having been exposed to it, found she was rooted in this particular geography for reasons she couldn't understand. The way the men moved, the gestures, all of it came with a rush of familiarity she hadn't anticipated. This feeling that brought her back to when she was twenty-two and traveled east across the front lines of the war in Croatia, in Karlovac where she had first seen buildings shot up from shelling, was overcome with nausea at the incessant need for human destruction. Sitting in the little apartment in Banja Luka with Katarina, she had understood that something in her made it comforting to be among shelled buildings, to be among people who'd had their worlds torn apart. But then she had settled in and bonded and sank into the humor and friendship, the smell of pepper mulch and cabbage leaves and sesame djevrek. Now she had come all the way through to the other side. To Carigrad. Istanbul. She had been imprinted like a baby bird. By a superior or inferior being, she wasn't sure. Perhaps it was a deep and powerful delusion, but to her it felt like home. She had learned Serbian, had learned Arabic, mostly, she could learn Turkish too. Knew half the words already. If it wasn't the sevdah of Bosnia it was the gumruk of Egypt. She just had to change her mumkin to mümkün, get used to the mellifluous pronunciation.

The adhan that was now the ezan resounded through the secular streets of Beyoğlu, echoing off the Turkcell vans, the boarded-up

British consulate, the renovated hotel where Agatha Christie and the Kennedys had stayed, and the strolling feet and arms and hands, the shirts and pants and scarves and skirts, the great mix of the city, which like the hectic streets of Cairo was calming, dunking her head in it, washing her brains of it, the heat of the soup, its mild saltiness, a cup of tea and a meander through the alleys until it was time to go home and stare at the ceiling, feeling dizzy and exhausted and hoping to sleep so deep that the migrations of her future would be washed away.

There was Alper and there was Eralp. There was Taner and there was Ertan. One man then another who stood behind or beside Laura when she stopped by the apartment downstairs. Sometimes one would stick around for a week or two, until he wanted too much, or was offended, or became aggressive, or left town—It's best when they leave town, Laura said—then she was alone briefly, swore everything off.

I call that one the Hummock, Laura said, returning to the white plastic table set out on the patch of concrete behind their building. She had a plate full of tomatoes and cheese in front of her, was about to eat a soft-boiled egg.—I thought I'd need the fire department to get him out of here.

It was an October noon just before the rains started, when the light fell like snow through the trees.

Tess had staggered back after a night in the apartment of some visiting artist from Europe. All the visiting artists. At a big slab of a wooden table, under a trellised shelter atop one of the old sloping buildings in Çukurcuma. Nights when Istanbul seemed to be teeming with comings and goings, with visiting artists from New York or Berlin and journalists back from Afghanistan and assessors or other contractors back from Libya or Bukhara. People not forbidden to move. Someone would have brought wine from the airport, much better and cheaper than what you could buy from the Tekel shop in the city, maybe packs of prosciutto or some other delicacy difficult to come by. Chitchat in several languages but rarely in Turkish, although someone new was always fascinated, trying to learn a word, thinking how interesting that *kayak* means *to ski* or something.

Tess went with Eren from the office. Eren with his soft-spoken relentlessness, his pointy elbows. They sat at the corner of the table, Eren's long arm around her as they shared a cigarette after the last of the good wine had been drunk.

Like her Eren was away from home. He came from a tiny village next to Van, not far from Iran. He'd hitchhiked with a friend to Antalya when he finished high school, and there he met a British gentleman who spoiled him for a week or two, changed his attitude about what he might do or be. My patron, Eren called him. With his patron's support he'd gone to the UK. Strangely, they were still in touch. The Englishman was living in a house on the south coast somewhere, a bay between Fethiye and Kaş, and working on a book about the intrigues of the Byzantine court, a historical telenovela in the form of a never-to-be-completed book. But very kind, very sweet. Eren owed him so much, he said. Only in his dotage he forgets things, he injures himself.—Last time I saw him he had a bandage on his forehead, Eren said. It's sad, when he visits, more than charming, as it always used to be. But still.

Now Eren lived in a little apartment in the same neighborhood as Tess and Laura, only further down in the Romani blocks at the bottom of the hill, where men load bricks and cinderblocks onto trucks and where children play plastic keyboards and boys dance in bedrooms, film themselves, and upload it to be shared, upswept gelled hair and pimples, dancing to some frenetic beats and harmonic minor wailing, crashing through the speakers. Eren was free to do as he pleased, to come and go as he pleased, and as he grew accustomed to the transgender women who made their home in his neighborhood, who sat in the teahouses playing cards without being bothered, and to the bars in the back alleys of Beyoğlu where boys and men sought each other openly, he felt that he could love who he pleased without worry.

Tess slid her body onto the ledge and sat with her back to the view, looking past Eren's half-smirk as he took in the scene of these foreigners, this alien Istanbul. Someone describing his fixer in Kabul, how they got past the checkpoint. A British journalist and her heavy-browed Kurdish photographer describing a trip to the Yazidi territories in Iraq.

Oh, the foreigners, Eren said.

It was good to feel this mutual exclusion, something shared. Tess watched his mischievous gaze, wondering who he was interested in, his bearing tranquil with the disappearing bottles.

Tess wandered downstairs to the kitchen, was pouring water from a pitcher when she noticed a pair of dark eyes, a body, one of these faces she ran into from time to time. A friend of a friend with an apartment overlooking the Golden Horn. She'd wanted nothing when she met him a few months ago, but then maybe. She thought she'd seen him on Istiklal, half-pretended to look away. Now he stood with a hand outstretched, his attentive fingers around a glass of wine.

It's not bad, he said. From a little farm in Thrace. We brought it back last week.

She accepted and lifted and swallowed and knew that she was no gentleman, and that she could not keep it clean like Laura, but still, uhhh. The need. Not for Abim and his patience. Not to bond but to gnash and press and pull. Eyes shut and mind blank for a second. Figure eights swirling across her body. Not giving a thought to the consequences. Letting that thirst take over for a second.

When she first worked in the camps in Macedonia, she found a pair of staffers in one of the latrines just mid-afternoon. She remembered the frail material of the woman's panties digging into her thigh, before Tess pressed the door closed to rid herself of the sight of them. And was returned to mud walkways between white tarps, lines of them off to the highway. Families and families and fucking in the middle of that.

An empty room in a stranger's flat. A bathroom somewhere. The solitude that was so delicious. Not danger or fear or power. Now it was just need pure and simple, muscles contracting, fistfuls of hair. Just don't look at me and don't talk to me afterward.

The summer before she left for Europe Tess had taken Amtrak to New Orleans and then to Chicago and hitchhiked to Maine and then down to New York. Young and foolish enough to subject herself to that, she thought, to think she needed it. The guy in Chicago, and on the train, and that couple who got her so stoned in New London, Connecticut, that she went back with them to their apartment. The girl made her feel safe at first, but once they were back there she realized how disoriented she was, and still there were those thirsts in her body, so confusing and powerful. The line between herself and others wasn't clear. Who or where she was. But she really had been there and really was herself, even in the blue sheets of that bedroom, pushing and clenching. The girl's breasts so helpless as she watched. Even more than fifteen years later a hot swell came to her when she thought about it. She could still feel the guy's hands on her. Pressing her cheek against the wall of the strange bedroom, that she walked out of later and into the streets not knowing what streets these were, still groggy from the grass and whiskey of comedown, and found a city bus to the Greyhound station and from there to Port Authority, arrived in New York with her head softened and more determined than ever to leave.

I love you, she remembered the streets of Zamalek, walking home before dawn. I love you I love you I love you.

She boiled water and made tea when she got up, happy to be alone in the garden with Laura in the October noon.

Did she even know why Laura first set off? Why they did it? Thinking they would find something in someone else's pain. Or that the pain of others would overwhelm their own. Or a simple thirst for adventure. Tess always thought of it as a kind of perfect stupidity, necessary in order to learn something terribly obvious. But there was also a luxury in it. Not the cars and expenditures of the organizations, the per diems and housing allowances, but the sense of wallowing in the world. Place after place after place. And her determination at the beginning that she was going to fight through it and be happy. Her happiness in Sarajevo and on her weekend trips to Belgrade, in the apartment in Bujanovac when she was first with Abim, when he first made her cups of Turkish coffee on his hotplate and they sat together still and silent, and his patience drove her mad, unfamiliar as it was.

Laura had always seemed larger and more physically powerful than the men around her, even if that made no sense. That bald merchant marine in Istanbul, sailing from Libya to Kotor to Cyprus to Istanbul. His head was so red and his eyes so huge and shaded. Ugly as sin, Laura said with a laugh. And all their bodies entwined, from Kansas City to Portland to Milan to Banja Luka, that first season in Bosnia. Entwined like Laura in heart monitor wires, thrashing and pressing. All of them pressing together. That particular loneliness. Waking up somewhere and feeling perfectly alone. Getting a new job somewhere and feeling perfectly alone. The blotches and discolorations and abrasions, imprints of car seats and sofas. That motherly feeling sometimes when they come. Yes, baby, that's it. A laugh in it, too, at their pride and vulnerability. All for this state that Laura was in, swollen and heaving, awash in these sweet and sour smells, the galloping heart of the unborn. Something that was in them, that spoke through them whether they wanted it to or not. A continuation of their own movement, from here to there to there. As Tess grew older and less deluded and learned to sit in one place and feel the navel of the world grow around her, newcomers would appear with the same hunger and ignorance, to scour and discard, to go out thinking they would find something, or get away from something, or become something. Tess in the green plastic chair could feel the heaviness of her hips, her sharp hipbones that pointed forward, her lower lip falling open. Laura on the hospital bed, thrashing heroically, this thrashing that ran through them. Even birth was a thrashing, squatting, rolling over, laying down, standing up, moving hips back and forth, pressing against something, pressing back against something. It was an amoebic form of reds and oranges and it was greater than her, inside and outside, working through her body, unthinking. Which is what made Tess go to Bosnia and Egypt and Turkey and was even why she was here with her friend. She needed to be here and needed to go there in order to be here. She was sure of that, watching Laura's face and her eyes shut and her mouth.

Tess welcomed a couple of potential donors from Sweden to the office. Tall, ironed, with crisp expressions. Tess introduced them to Eren and Omar, then led them to the back where they could chat until the meeting began.

Laura had been flustered and overwhelmed all morning, but she stepped in with her hair up and out of her face and her bearing calm. When she answered their questions she was focused, professional.— Some 20,000 migrants now assigned to 25 satellite cities in Central Anatolia.—The pair of consultants dispatched from the Nordic Council wanted to provide PiF with equipment: new computers, for example, or video cameras.—Of course what we need are operating funds, Laura said. We use the computers we have to fill out forms. Excel, Word, email, that's all we need. But we have to pay our translators and our legal advisors.

I'm afraid we can't—

I'm aware of your limitations, but I want you to know what we actually need, so that we can find a way to work together that isn't counterproductive.

What about psychosocial activities?

I'm a big advocate for psychosocial, but we're discussing situations where food, shelter, and freedom from deportation are pressing concerns. Psychosocial services require stable conditions.

I'm only mentioning the sectors where we have a budget.

I understand that.

Laura sat, smiled, glared at these two men, one blond, one dark-haired, in their striped shirts and dark trousers, with their expensive and tasteful eyeglasses, the blond with a gold wedding band on his left ring finger.

We specialize in building capacity among local partner organizations. We provide equipment and training to use new technology, for example.

Yes? Laura looked at him expectantly.

We provided an organization in Addis Ababa with a basic production set-up, and they used it to interview refugees from the south of Ethiopia.

IDPs, Laura corrected.

Excuse me?

Internally displaced persons. They're not refugees. They're still in their home country. They have the right to work legally, to access medical care. I've never been to Ethiopia. I don't know what the conditions are, but it's a distinct set of issues.

In any case—

I just want you understand.

We do understand. I'm explaining.

You don't understand the difference between an asylum seeker, a refugee, and an IDP, but these are all distinct situations requiring distinct tactics. There are different legal classifications, different procedures, the UNHCR processes them in different ways. It's somewhat complex, but not difficult to understand. All you need to do is review a document that can be accessed on a ten-year-old computer hooked up to a modem, or you can pick up the phone and call the UNHCR rep in your country, or any country.

The blond was now taking a deep breath.

We're here to look for ways to collaborate.

Yes, and obviously we're looking for any support we can get. However, I want you to forget your line items, your mandate, what you think you came here for. I want you to listen, and to understand the situation. If you want I can arrange for you to talk to asylum seekers all afternoon, and they will tell you all about the problems they face. You can also trust me, because I do this every day.

We have a lot of respect for what—

Of course you do, and I know that you're here to help, so I want you to learn a little about what we do, and what we're facing, so that your assistance will not be wasted.

What's your proposal?

But it was Tess who began to speak, her voice emerging dry from her throat, certain of what she was going to tell them:

It sounds to me that the organization in need of capacity building is yours.—Laura turned to look at her.—You should hire us as consultants, offering training. You send staff from your organization, pay for their housing, and we'll train them to provide legal assistance to migrants in Turkey. When they've developed that capacity, they can provide legal assistance like we do. If they're interested in staying, they can apply for funding for permanent positions.

But that is—

Listen, Laura now piped in, having instantly grasped Tess's argument. All the late-night discussions they'd had, all the polite talk with donors:

This is one of the prime entry points for migrants to the European Union. Once they cross the river into Greece, it becomes a European problem. But that problem is already here. So by understanding the situation here, you will be better able to advocate rational policies in Europe. You will have what is called field experience, and that is invaluable in creating policy. If you have no field experience, you will come here trying to implement policies that may or may not have worked in the horn of Africa, and that is a level of incompetence much worse than out-of-date technology.

The blond now changed his position in his chair:

I want you to—

I know, Laura went on. I know you do. But listen. We're telling you something that will help us, because we will have, at least temporarily, a few more legal advisors that we don't have to pay for, which will allow us to work through our caseload. We're backed up here. Hundreds of cases. Just yesterday we had to send staff to Ataturk airport with emergency forms to halt a deportation of twelve Afghan nationals. We have a collective center in Kadıköy that houses several hundred unaccompanied minors, that may or may not be closed by the interior ministry next month. We have ten Central African migrants sleeping in the attic of an Episcopalian church around the corner. We have a situation on the border with Syria that no one knows where it's headed.

She paused for a second and Tess turned to them with a shrug:

You'll have to decide whether your goal is to go back to Stockholm with a digestible report for your superiors, or whether your goal is to learn to adapt to situations, to listen and respond, and to have a chance of not making things worse.

By ten o'clock they were sitting in an alleyway off Istiklal, with dozens of empty plates in front of them, the last remnants of sardines and liver, of garlic-boiled seagrasses and pistachio halva, smoking Rothmans from the Stockholm airport and drinking rakı without water. Laura now pulled out her chair and got up. Tess watched her climb on top of the table, squat there with her shoes between the empty plates. Laura bunched up her skirt, pressed her palms down on her knees, and pissed. She pissed out all the forms and reports and

148

information requests and extensions and follow-up grant proposals and ROAs and tax documents that had ever passed through her fingers, so it all poured from the tabletop onto the concrete alley off Istiklal, seeped into the sewer and ran down to the Bosporus and then the Marmara and the Mediterranean, dissolving into the soup the dolphins leapt through at the Gates of Hercules. Then she reached over to plant a big muscled kiss on each of the pliant mouths of these visitors from the West.

Laura pressed her hips back against Tess's body as Tess tried to squeeze them together, bone against bone against muscle against body, and there in that motion, in those fluids that rushed and gushed inside her, the amniosis and peristalsis of her situation, were not only the Istanbul nights at the end of days, and mornings the next morning practically running over the hill to the office, but the manic drives through the Balkans they'd made the summer they first met, the dives into Lake Ohrid way up in the Macedonian mountains, with the prehistoric trout with its delicate pink flesh, dance parties in the caves along the Albanian border, where grandmothers dragged bushels of marijuana out of their attics, sold to the driver of their organization, squeezed into sausage-shaped bundles of brown paper and electrical tape, thrown into the trunk of their white 4x4, sold and distributed around Skopje and Tetovo and Gostivar, the boredom of government briefings and the hypocrisy of plenary sessions, the statistics of small-arms trading from Egypt to Sudan, the planeloads of ammunition landing at Marsa Alam before it was turned into a resort, the solitary soldiers guarding Sufi tombs in the Western desert, the lonely European women hunting Bedu in the Sinai, the Land Rovers through Burundi before Tess met her, all of that swelled and gushed inside her, was what her body was made of, as much as her father's lemon-yellow suit and her mom's sepia fruitstand. And whatever Barish saw when he saw her, what he embraced when he embraced her, was that, all of that, too. It was all in the soft flesh of her inner arms, the lines around her eyes that had deepened since her mom died, since she found out she was pregnant, since she decided she would be a mother, since she sat with the boxes of photos and letters and artifacts from the past of her parents, from high school in Brooklyn, from summer camp in Massachusetts, trips to visit her Mexican grandparents in La Florida, in that house of empty rooms she had described to Tess, with the very small woman who dusted the plates and statues and shelves of books that no one ever touched, the windows out onto the rectangular garden, the statue of a goldfish spitting water out of its puckered lips, the bougainvillea spilling over the high walls that separated them from others, where Laura lay as a girl through the cool nights looking straight up at the sky, the occasional star that could be seen through the pollution, thinking of the volcanoes nearby that would puff smoke, the male and female volcanoes there, living together forever, while she lay in the backyard of her grandparents' house, every summer until she grew up and went away and kept leaving and leaving until she found herself leaning over her mother's dying body, thinking that she hadn't even been there for her grandparents' deaths, and wondered what her father was doing in that house in Mexico City, if he was still there, wondering what he would think about being a grandfather, only child of an only child of an only child. All of what Tess squeezed when she squeezed Laura's hips, what Barish held up when he grabbed her by the armpits, when her hair draped over his shoulder, when they clung together the three of them in the darkened room of the delivery ward, squeezing and straining and trying to make something happen, which no one knew what, or why. Laura as a baby coming out of her mother in Cuernavaca, with the heated towels, always hotter, having been born of those heated towels, so that her own child would know of Tess, of her friend who had squeezed her hips when the contractions came. But then no one thought of that, or remembered things like that. What did Tess know? And what was inside her? Her mother in Research Hospital, where Bess Truman wasted away the year before or after, she heard, her mother on drugs or not on drugs, she didn't know. Her negligent, two-timing father probably not even there, hearing about it later, her and her sister in that little house up the road from the art museum, then her own endless series of departures and friendships and departures, squeezing Laura's hips, her arms aching, but still squeezing with all her strength, her face hot, having never worked so hard in her life. They weren't kidding when they called it labor. But at least she could move away at the end of the contraction, go back to that green plastic chair and drop.

But instead of exhaustion now Tess felt a burst of appetite. How hungry she was all of the sudden. And Laura must be too. Was Laura allowed to eat? She must be starving. Tess by herself could eat a steak or a plate of pasta or at least a sandwich. Wasn't there somewhere she could get some food? Barish, he'd have to keep things under control. It's the middle of the night, right. The graveyard shift. But there has to be something. If this is going to go on much longer, which it seems like it will.

I've got to go downstairs for a second, she said to Laura, catching her breath after another contraction. I think I remember seeing a diner or something across the street from the hospital. I'm going down for some food.

Laura looked at her without speaking, her chest rising and falling, her lips limp and somehow swollen.

You're going to leave me alone?

Just for a few minutes.

Barish didn't say anything.

I've got to get something. I'm dying here.

Laura let out a short sharp laugh.

Fuck off, Tess said, despite herself. Then corrected: I'm sorry.

But Laura was just laughing, or sobbing. No, laughing. It must be laughing.

The antiseptic hallway was perfectly light and distant. Nothing for her to do. The darkness of the birthing room, the gravity of Laura's need had been pulling on her, dragging her in, and now she was released. She stood at the exit to the labor and delivery ward, waiting for the nurse to buzz open the exit doors, and when the doors opened she walked out of the ward, her steps light and her arms weightless.

What was the difference, anyway, between this trip to the Skotos Diner and all her trips to the satellite cities, or up the Nile, or to the forgotten villages of the south Balkans? She stood in the elevator, which was as large and lonely as the departures hall of an airport.

The doors opened a few floors down, and a nurse pushed in a gurney, on which was a man draped in hospital fabric, squirming and emitting coughing sounds from his obscured face. The elevator seemed to move with excruciating slowness as the man tried to move right and left. Tess watched the nurse stare at the numbers that marked their descent: 7, 6, 5. Every night another wounded man, another sick and hopeless man. Rolling a man through the hallways. Rolling a woman into the operating theater. Dressing wounds, applying anesthetic, changing bedpans.

The labor and delivery nurses were lucky, Tess thought. Everyone went home happy, or almost everyone, she supposed. Now and then there must be a tragedy. A mother or a baby dies, or is born ill or with some unforeseen irregularity. Can it happen, Tess thought, in a way that you're unprepared for? That you give birth to a malformed little creature. You had no idea but instead of a little conehead blue baby out comes a baby with limbs in some extraordinary place, or with porcupine quills or whiskered like a cat. You accidentally give birth to a crocodile or a panda or a set of tiny office furniture. What would you do?

My babies, she imagined herself cradling such creatures.

The elevator doors opened on the third floor and the nurse rolled the injured man out into the hallway, hiccupping and squirming, not knowing where he was. Helpless as a child, Tess thought. Two other hospital staffers entered the elevator mid-conversation. Something about the new doctor, or a man at least, Tess couldn't tell.

She exited the elevator and stood for a second in the hallway, unsure where to go. It was so late now that the main entranceway was closed. She walked in circles for a second before finding the entrance to the emergency room. A bored guard at a kiosk pointed toward a set of sliding doors.

Tess found herself on 58th St, in the middle of the block. Bare brick walls and garbage. Trucks parked across the street. But even this late at night the weather was still beautiful, cool and comfortable. She was happy to breathe the air that swept through the city for a second. She walked to the left and circled around the main entrance to the hospital, now locked and dark in the middle of the night. But there on the corner was a little hospital deli. *10% off with hospital ID*, said a sign. She could see two or three people seated in the dining area, most with hospital scrubs on. She walked in and took a seat.

It was nearly 2 AM. She picked up the laminated menu and stared at it. Reuben, pastrami on rye, turkey potpie, Belgian waffle, gyros, challah French toast. All of it terrible and overpriced, she thought, and ordered a plate of steak and eggs for here.

Medium, she said. Eggs scrambled. With rye toast.

She folded the menu and handed it to the waiter, a swarthy fellow who spoke with soft and buzzing s's. She imagined he'd just come over from Larissa or something. Having known his uncle who returns to Greece each summer, but never thinking he'd take him up on his offer to come work for him. Hard to imagine he was happy to be here, she thought. But the crisis in Greece, once again, just like before.

Coffee, she said. Cream no sugar. And a bottle of seltzer if you have one.

It felt good to say those things: *cream no sugar*. American things. She knew how to say the words.

The waiter walked off and she looked at the hair on the back of his neck. Black hair, Balkan hair. Somewhere behind the counter she could see a flame shoot up from the grill. A huge grease fire and they'd all go up in a round ball of flame. *Fuwwwaaah*.

Hey, she called to the waiter. Could you bring me a cheese danish to eat while I wait?

He smiled and nodded and turned back to what he was doing. She sat back in her chair and looked around at the room, at the hospital staffers having a coffee break, at the corner of 10th Ave. People working night and day, day and night.

The cheese danish was cold and stale and overly sweet, just as she'd imagined. It dissolved into crumbs around her mouth and the paper placemat in front of her was covered in bad pastry bits, which she swept aside and gathered with her napkin. She remembered Chubby's Diner on 39th St in Kansas City, where she used to sit in high school. A room of black-and-white-checkered tiles and neon lights. Her mother's house still the last place she'd lived in the US. The only place, actually. Chubby's Diner used to seem from another time, she thought. A little romantic. Now she realized that it was just where she was from. That was it. Like this. American, she thought, looking at the Greeks and Mexicans behind the counter.

She sat for a second thoughtless, exhausted, and in a way, perfectly satisfied. Not wondering where to go or what to be, just seated in her chair in the light of the diner, her stomach grumbling for steak and eggs.

Barish and Laura and the baby, she thought. And this is Aunt Tess. She huffed, not happy about the way that sounded. But still, imagined the eyes of a child taking her in, years later, walking and talking and looking out from eyes possessed of their own native intelligence, having forgotten Tess from the time she was born, of course. Who is this person? The child or me?

She could smell the food cooking behind the counter. That cheap oil they used on the grill. It smelled fantastic. The waiter came to her with a huge plate full of food, which she ate with gleeful concentration, looking up only to say:

Another order, the same, but to-go. And two coffees.

By the time she had finished he was back with a plastic bag full of styrofoam to-go packaging, little cellophane packets of ketchup and mustard, coffees in tall paper cups, with extra cream in tiny plastic sealed buckets. All of it seemed to her things from the past. She was comforted to know any of that still existed. She paid the extravagant bill, and grabbed a cardboard matchbook on the way out.

Tess walked. She felt good walking. She had always walked. In Istanbul she walked endlessly up and down the steep slopes of Beyoğlu. She navigated the steep hills of Galata down to the waterfront, looking to arrange a boat for an excursion on the Golden Horn. She needed to escort some reps from a donor agency around the city, show them a fabulous time. She wandered down to the teahouse at the end of the machine parts market, where they park the ferries when they're not in use.

The owner of the teahouse was a tiny fellow named Mehmet Abi, who served tea to the boatworkers, repairmen, dealers in acetone and iron scrap. It reminded her of Belgrade, of the riverfront where Max had spent all his time during their years in Serbia. The Dorćol marina, the old tugboat in the fairgrounds, the rugged happiness of men and women who loved the water as their own, the Danube, the Sava, the Golden Horn, even Nasreddin and Safiya on the Nile, part of the same way of life.

She asked Mehmet Abi if he knew anyone who could take her donors out for a few hours.

He stuck his fingers in his mouth and whistled and up came Selim. Tanned and muscled, with a strong jaw and short chestnut-colored waves, he listened to what she said, pulled out his phone, said something quickly and hung up. He led her down to one of the docks out into the jellyfish-ridden waters and they stood looking across the Horn at Sultanahmet, the skyline of the old city. The delicate minarets of the Yeni Camii in front of the spice market and the Rüstem Paşa

Camii perched in the middle of Tahtakale, where you could buy oak barrels to age brandy, aluminum flues for your pot-bellied stove, dried hibiscus and leather hats.

She could feel the nearness of Selim's upper arms, their sinew and strength. She was taller than him, she realized, and older. Just a boy, she thought as the boat arrived, and then thought: Who have I become?

The boat was a bobbing double-decker. When it was close she could see Bekir the captain with his crazed look, his missing teeth, his own arms covered everywhere in a hatchwork of scars. Bekir let the boat idle by the dock and Selim jumped on board, held on to the dock while Tess scrambled in too, and they set off back across the Horn.

The bottom deck was hung with scuba-diving suits. Selim explained that he and Bekir were professional divers. They get called in to work on tankers and container ships, they can perform repairs without pulling the boats out of the water. But they have this boat too and on weekends they take people out to the uninhabited islands in the Marmara, teach them how to dive.

There are Byzantine and Genoese ships still at the bottom of the Marmara, he said. You should come with us.

Fine, Tess said, and looked into his crazed eyes, his euphoria that dwelled free and easy on the water.

Which led to the afternoon with Laura. Bekir with a big crumbling joint in his mouth as he sped out of the Bosporus into the open sea of the Marmara, the Asian shores of the city slowly receding, a haze of ugly developments off to the horizon, as they left behind the endless tankers parked at the mouth of the straits, what Tess had seen on the way from the airport when she first landed in the city. Ship after ship waiting to enter the international waterway to the Black Sea, just like the truckers backed up at the border between Macedonia and Kosovo. Waiting to visit the whorehouses in Aksaray, Tess guessed, to hand over wages for the bodies of refugee girls from Iraq and Afghanistan, sisters of the men who came to them at PiF.

They pulled away from the usual ferry path to the Prince's Islands, from the Armenian weekend houses and crowded beaches of Kınalıada, and headed west toward the small island called Yassıada. Tess had seen it many times from the ferry. It had always looked to her like the head of a giant frog peeking out from the sea.

Bekir pulled into a small bay on the south side of the island, and Tess could see a concrete dock built into the shore. When they got closer, Selim jumped off the deck onto the dock and Bekir threw him a rope to tie them up. Those effortless movements. A good thing for a man to do, Tess thought. Tie up a boat. She watched Selim's muscled arms as they worked, with grace and speed, spiraling around the iron tie.

Before they got ready to dive, Selim led them up onto the island, up toward the rectangular buildings that were the eyes of the frog. The island was uninhabited, visiting it was forbidden, so as they ascended they passed through the Marmara landscape in something like its natural state. Mulberry brambles and tiny wild figs, raging bushes and flowers, extraterrestrial succulents reaching up to the sky, and the garland of waters extending in all directions. Even with the sea full of tankers and ferries, jellyfish and sludge, here there was a glimpse of the original paradisiacal home. Laura and Bekir ran up ahead and Selim and Tess caught up with them at the entrance to an abandoned building, an old university or military installation, all of its windows broken. Bekir led them inside and they wandered up the huge staircase until they got to the roof. Bekir burst out onto the concrete surface, a huge rectangle, the giant frog's right eyeball, where they could look out over the wild growth below.

Selim told her the Marmara here was thirty meters lower than the Black Sea, so the Bosporus had always been pouring downhill. That's why it's so treacherous, and that permanent gush is what gave the city its freshness, why the air was so particular. Always too cold or too hot, but somehow delicious. But once the gush hit the openness of the Marmara, it calmed. The compact forces expanded and settled. The sea traffic from China to Russia. Dolphins on their way from the Sea of Azov to the Atlantic. The entire world contained in this single frog's eyeball. In a different way than the tree behind Hamed's house in Sasida. A different, more openly manifest navel. Everyone came here. Everyone had been here. And it was only increasing. Not only asylum seekers and migrants from Congo and Iran, tourists from the Gulf and the West, but more and more ships and submarines and ferries. The skies were once blacked out with dense flights of birds. Now Tess watched the scanty hordes of evil seagulls diving into the bay below, perhaps coming up with the petrified fingernail of a ninth-century sailor from Genoa or Tyre, the gull flying with the sliver of horn in its red-eyed beak up to the top of the Sapphire tower back in Şişli, an unfinished skyscraper, ugly, destined to be uglier, a testament to what the city was becoming.

Back at shore Bekir tossed them each a tank and a mask and very quickly disappeared underwater. Tess watched Laura confidently strap on her gear and go underwater too, while she, gingerly, with instructions from Selim, sunk down to the bottom.

The waters were filthy, there was nothing visible. All the Byzantine ships of the past had been dissolved into a thick cloud of murk and bubbles. It was like the lead ball she carried in her chest, rich and toxic, a nauseating slime made from the waste of the world. Tess floated in the polluted amniosis and imagined the city above and everywhere, sucking all the industrial and human and animal waste from the river basins of Europe and Asia and dumping it into this beautiful spot.

And feeling that, she wanted to open her mouth and start to swallow, to take in all the jellyfish, the poisoned tabby-fish, the invisible schools of bonito and the last lonely octopus. It would all come into her and cool her and meet her skin from within, until she was still and silent like the air in the aluminum elevator, exactly the same temperature as the water.

I can't, Laura cried. I can't do it.

Tess pushed in the door with her shoulder and found Barish behind Laura. Laura was again bent over so she could rest her forearms on the hospital bed. Again her ass was in Tess's face, her muscled vulva and splotchy thighs. The green-and-white pads laid out on the tile floor. The smell of it all enveloped Tess's head until she was dizzy from it. The rubbing alcohol and stainless steel hospital smells, then a loamy, shit-and-blood smell that must have been Laura's body fluids and hormones. It was all low notes and almost beautiful, like a dank forest floor where things were rotting and growing at the same time.

Barish had taken his jacket off and was rubbing Laura's lower back, pushing down with both hands as she arched her spine and then pushed her hips forward, arched and pushed. Barish struggling to keep the pressure even with his two hands. The smell must have risen slowly, Tess thought, so that they hadn't noticed. She had to go out and come back to feel it.

Aaaaaah, Laura said.

Just let it go, let it go, Barish said.

Tess shut the door and walked in, stood in the middle of the room with the bag of food in her hand.

Oh God, that smells terrible. Laura moaned as she continued to work her hips forward and back. Oh God, Tess, get that out of here.

Tess stood motionless, not responding to her request.

Barish looked at her as he continued to struggle.

Just a second, he said. Hold on.

It wasn't clear who he was talking to.

Tess moved around them and plopped down into the green plastic chair and set the bag of food on the floor next to her. Then she stood up and took off her jacket, the light fall jacket she'd pulled on to go outside. Again she was in the flimsy striped shirt she'd thrown on that morning, that Laura had complimented back when she was semi-coherent. She sat back down in the chair and waited for the contraction to be over, for Laura to hit the lowering mechanism on the bed, to climb back up on the mattress and lay on her side whimpering. But when it was over Laura continued to moan and cry, as if the contraction hadn't really ended. She made pale, whimpering sounds, sallow and pathetic. Tess looked at her face, squinched up in pain.

You should eat something, Tess said.

Bllleaaaaagh, Laura sputtered between shallow exhalations.

The nurse says she shouldn't, Barish said.

Tess shrugged and pulled out the styrofoam container and set it on the countertop at the end of the bed to the left of the baby warmer, above the biohazard receptacle.

Here, she said to Barish, and lay down a package with a knife and fork and napkin.

Ahh-huh-ahh-huh-aaaaaah, Laura said. I'm so tired.

Barish opened the top of the styrofoam container and looked down at his steak and eggs.

My God, he said.

He unpacked his utensils and took a bite of eggs.

It's good, eh? Tess said.

You are all disgusting, Laura said, still whimpering.

Barish sawed at the steak with his plastic fork and stuck a bite into his mouth in silence, leaning over the biohazard countertop. Tess held her second coffee between her thighs on the green chair. The curved plastic head and insect eye of the baby warmer between them.

You can't do that again, Tess, okay?

Laura had caught her breath but still seemed sunk in self-pity.

Okay, Tess said, taking a swallow of coffee. I won't. I promise.

The door to the room popped open and in came Nurse Joanne. She flipped on the light switch and they were again stung by the harsh white overhead light. Tess looked up, squinting, but Barish was unfazed and continued to shovel steak and ketchup into his whiskered face.

Bon appetit! The nurse cackled over her red plastic reading glasses. Gathering steam for the good part, I guess.

She walked to the workstation and checked the monitor, then turned to face Laura.

I bet the smell bothers you, doesn't it?

Laura wrinkled up her face and stuck out her tongue like a little girl. Tess imagined the nurse must get high off the loamy smells of birth.

You should really take that out of here. You might make mama nauseous. How you doing, hon?

Laura just nodded and didn't say anything.

· Fine, Barish said, and gathered up his styrofoam container, his knife and fork. I'll be back in a second.

The nurse opened the door for him and shut it again behind him. She turned back to Laura with a smile on her face, apparently pleased to have him gone.

That's better now, isn't it? She spoke over her red reading glasses, a brown beaded lanyard disappearing under her frosted hair.

Thank you, nurse. Really, Laura said, rolling over on her side, clutching her belly.

The nurse walked to her and patted her on the thigh, laughed briefly, then turned to grab the thermometer from the desktop. She shook it once or twice and opened her mouth, Laura imitated her, and the nurse popped the thing in.

Tess tossed her empty coffee cup into the trashcan, and the nurse turned to her.

How you doing, hon?

Much better. I had some food and I'm ready.

Well don't get too excited, we've still got a ways to go, the nurse said.

Laura blurted something incomprehensible, clutched her belly and groaned. Not from pain, Tess thought. Just from the thought that she had to keep going.

I should have asked for drugs, Laura said when the nurse grabbed the thermometer out of her mouth.

A wave now swept over her and she began to cry and make low animal noises again. Tess stood over her and pressed down on the hip that was facing up.

Yes, please, Tess, yes, that's it. More. Aaaaauuuuurrrhh.

The nurse stood and watched what Tess was doing.

I can see you've got everything under control, she said to Tess. I'll be back in a while to check on you.

The nurse turned off the lights as she went out the door.

Nurse, Tess called after her, hoping to ask a question, but she was already gone.

One of those nights walking back to Aynalı Çeşme with Laura, those steep hills, Tess lay down on the street on her back, arms out, feeling a ridiculous euphoria spread through her body, some echo of the giddiness she began to feel when she was alone in Cairo after Abim's departure.

Get up, loca, you'll get killed.

Laura laughing, grabbing her wrist, and the two of them staggering back to their building, to dissolve each in their own bed, on their own floor, in their own solitude, finally at the end of it. There was none of Abim's divinity here, not even if the streets were named after dead Sufis. The neighborhood was of this world, concrete and stone and houses and bad beer and the bullet-hole hangovers of the rakı, so different from the clarifying sting of the rakija of the Balkans. Here instead of clarity it was a sweetness that turned cloudy when you add water, and that cloud was in you, that sugary fleece. Tess on her back on the street. How long could it last?

Until she woke up to find a fat envelope in the mailbox in her hallway, an old-fashioned pen-and-paper letter from her brother Max, sent from his mountaintop, written in his cave of a cell.

He told her of his periodic trips to Damascus, where he sat with a bookseller friend in the old city, an expert in American literature who'd been fired from the university for opposing the regime. He described a recent trip to Beirut where he'd stayed with Abim, where he'd seen Abim looking happy and hard at work, very adjusted to life in Beirut. It was one of the last days of Ramadan, and though Abim wasn't fasting they'd gone together to a friend's apartment, sat on the balcony to break the fast at the end of the day. The cacophony of the prayers, the shouted sermons above the Shi'a neighborhood, rifles fired into the air after a televised speech by Hassan Nasrallah.

Abim very comfortable there, Max said. But what Tess liked best was the part about not fasting. Perhaps he's changing, she thought.

But Max. What had happened to him?

Max had stood next to her when she shook out the container of ashes in San Francisco. They'd talked on the phone a lot after that. It was the only thing that helped. Then their conversations grew more infrequent, and when she'd turned up at his apartment in New York two years later, she found the place littered with empty wax paper packets. While she was struggling to finish college and wandering aimlessly along US two-lanes, Max had been sucking more and more cream-colored heroin into his nostrils. He said if he hadn't followed her to Bosnia, he was doomed. He'd taken one hit with another junkie in Sarajevo, and Tess thought he would descend right back. Post-war Sarajevo was awash with narcotics. Like in New York, dealers gave out bags of dust for free, to make sure they had a stable of addicts. But Max and his friend both kicked, while spending months editing and archiving war footage, rendering masses of clips into exquisite, unwatchable ten-minute films.

He was lucky. But she realized he had been lost and confused all along. Since they first met as kids. She was too young to realize. She and her sister were his only friends. His miserable mother in that suburban house, serial killer neighbors burying bones in their backyards. The Christian fanatics at his high school. Now he was the fanatic.

She wondered if she and Max would ever be as close as they'd been in Bosnia and Serbia, or the summer after they'd fled the chaos and corruption of Kosovo to jump into the dark blue Aegean at the end of the Cyclades, when they'd been caught in the Athens earthquake and slept all night on the Acropolis, sharing some silence at that time.

Now he was back to his Syrian monastery, to the Jesuit's booming voice, visiting schoolchildren, a cot in a cave, rising early to prepare the morning meal, sweep floors, milk goats, help one of the sisters make cheese, before wandering up to his abandoned peaks and his inward spiral. It was just like the packets of cream-colored dusts from Attorney Street, she thought.

What could a person learn in that inward space? Tess suspected it was a falsehood, an attempt to conceive of oneself as the sole source of consciousness, but Max found it meaningful.

A node in the center of the head, he described, just above the roof of the mouth, that when activated becomes receptive: intuition, inspiration, messages from somewhere. Concentrating while walking, he began to feel it like a physical sensation. The dot: colorless, unmoving, but pulsing somehow with breath. In, out, in, out. Pulsing with a periodicity of four beats per breath. As he walked, the sound of the wind. Until the wind also pulsed at four beats per breath.

It was his antidote to the lead ball, the juice of waste that hung at Tess's chest, that burrowed into her and nestled in her hips, that contained everything that happened to her, all of it cooked down to a thick and toxic broth.

If I could empty my head of memories, Max wrote, and just feel footsteps. Yes, she thought. That must be it. Max had come to the end of the road, monastic life, the medieval precipice, among the holy fools of the Syrian deserts. Not to have to make decisions, to decide what to say or do, but just follow instructions, and when there was nothing to do, to walk among the treeless peaks. They were linked, she thought, even if his way was so different. Max could wander the barren hills. It was just fine. Feeling the dot above the roof of his mouth swell and pulse.

For months she heard nothing from him. Until another letter came telling her that he was about to move from the monastery to a hermit cave further up the mountain, and he would only come down once a week.

A hermit had lived there, he wrote, but the hermit had gone away.

Max met him once, an Englishman, even occasionally spent the night up there, talking to the English hermit.

Tess imagined these talks like the talks with Nasreddin on the houseboat. Always heading to that hermit cave above the monastery, an end to free will.

The hermit left without notice. Max had stopped by the cave and it had been evacuated, so he asked the Jesuit if he could move in. But the Jesuit had no sway up there, he told him. He was on his own.

Imagine, he wrote, a place in the world where no one has any sway.

There was a Christian named Simon, he wrote at the end of the letter, who used to hunt around for scorpion pits to lie in. Later he climbed up a pole twenty feet high in order to be closer to God. It sounds stupid, Max said, but when he was up there, he felt it. And he never wanted to come down. He stood up on top of the pole. People handed food to him. He slept there, shat there, stayed until he died there.

Max alone among the stones. Walking and sitting. What happens, he wanted to know, if there is no input?

What Tess wanted to know was what happened to the guy on the pole's shit? Did it fall from his ass twenty feet in the air to plop in a pile on the ground? Did his followers gather it and bake it into coin-sized discs to be sold to pilgrims?

But there was no return address, no way to ask or respond.

From Johnson County to junkiedom to wandering the Syrian desert, she thought: Max.

Why did they do what they did? Any of them. Why did Max

want to be alone like that? And what about her? She remembered standing at the Kosovo border, the bodies in no man's land, the first real emergency she'd been caught in. The shock and confusion when she realized half the people she'd thought were exhausted and resting were in fact dead. Nothing was real until that new lens fell into place. Then with the change of vision her pulse jumped, the smell of death hit her, and her mind went blank. She and Laura were left to coordinate with the Red Cross, to call in medics and transport for the survivors, to evacuate the bodies. She returned to the lines of white tarp tents of the refugee camp, swelling fast once the borders were reopened, with no idea what was going on around her.

Tess sat back in the green plastic armchair and for the first time in a while she noticed the sound of the baby's heart. There it is. That's what all this has led to. Laura's kid.

How many babies were born in that patch of mud that summer, or in the refugee camps? All the cries echoing through the lanes of white tarps, all the marriages, humanitarian staffers fucking in portable toilets, carnival rides at the edge of the camp, prostitution rings inside it. All of us are like that, Tess thought. We crab and bicker and betray each other, scrounging for scraps from ration packs. She looked out the window and the buildings in the neighborhood surrounding them were just another form of refugee camp, white tarps stacked up to the sky, people chasing scraps as if they were huge golden prizes. And soon the tents will collapse, the tarps will fall, and we'll fall down and die in the mud, writhe and give birth in the mud.

Laura moved as if irritated, unable to find the right position, now she was up on her knees again, and Tess stood up so she could support her from behind, Laura's head back on her shoulder, face clenched shut.

You're doing great, Tess began to speak without realizing it. Let it move through you, she said. Just like that.

I can't do it. Laura writhed and cried. I'm weak.

You're huge. Tess said. You're enormous.

I'm a baby, Laura said. I'm a little baby. I can't do this.

Think about Skopje, Tess said. Remember the border with Kosovo.

When the Macedonians shut the border and we were there with all those people in the mud.

Aaaaaah, Laura said.

The rain was falling and there was that line of people backed up into the forest and there were helicopters and soldiers around us.

Tess didn't know what she was doing, but even if Laura couldn't, at least she could picture it. How could Laura be weak?

Remember the Italian cop we talked to in front of the Stenkovec camp? Carabinieri or something except he had that shiny green feather in his helmet. Remember! We were asking him what the Macedonians told them, and you were speaking to him in Spanish and he answered in Italian, saying he didn't know anything. In his feathered helmet. Remember?

I remember, Laura said.

That little man that came out from the ministry trying to explain why he couldn't open the border. We told him to fuck himself, remember? I didn't even know what I was saying but I kept cursing at him in Serbian. I don't know what I could have been saying.

Jebem ti sunce! Laura said. *Jebem ti majko!*

Exactly! Tess said. He couldn't believe it. Two American humanitarian women telling him to fuck his mother, in Serbian!

Laura's moan turned into a smile and a laugh wracked her body for a second.—I remember!—Then she dissolved into screams, gripping Tess's forearms until she would cut off the circulation.

He kept telling us how he was going to open the border, Tess said, but then he didn't, and then the rains came and people were dropping dead.

That was the real catastrophe, Laura said. All we could do was watch them die.

Until you followed the minister into his press conference and brought up the situation in front of all the international news agencies. Then it was big news.

Thank god, Laura asked. They were dying right in front of us.

Right, then the motorcade out to the border and him with his fat ass right from the ministry gave a speech and finally let us through into no man's land so we could bring people food and medicine.

I was so crazy! Laura said. I could have killed every single one of them.

I know, Tess said. Me too. But it was you. You did it!

For some of them, it's true, she said, gasping for air. But the field was full of bodies.

Tess remembered. The rains let up and then the flies came. The sick and wounded who turned out to be dead. Carrying away bodies, lifting them onto stretchers and carrying them to the truck. The sun now baking everything. She had never smelled anything like it. Laura was walking through like a victorious general, ordering people around.

But more people would have died if you hadn't done that, Tess said. You saved them.

Laura sat up now on the hospital bed, breathing hard, clutching her belly. Tess looked into her eyes to see where she was. Was she here? Laura turned back and returned her stare, wide-eyed, afraid—Oh God, Tess. Thank you for being here—and she collapsed onto her side and started whimpering.

I can't believe that's her, Tess thought, looking down at her. That's really her. Ten years later. More than ten. Twelve, fifteen years later. That was already her, Tess thought. She was my hero. And now look at her. She was just a kid, then. I didn't realize. We were so young! Twenty-five-year-old kids caught up in that war. And Laura was so brave, she thought. And no one will ever know.

And you got fired because of it, Laura said to Tess.

Not because of that, Tess said. But yeah, I got fired.

The bitterness of the end of that summer rose up in her throat. Not only the asshole minister, their racist landlords and all the Macedonian Slavs and Albanians that wanted to kill each other, but the Americans, the NATO patrols, the Australian procurement officer with his silver BMW stolen somewhere in Europe, bragging about his Bosnian plates. Imagine, Tess thought, him proud of his Bosnian plates. A fucking car thief.

Adrenaline surged through her and she relaxed her fists now. Laura was no longer pressing her hands into her pelvis. And for a moment they could relax and breathe and forget about the past. Why did I bring that up? Tess thought. What good is it to remember any of that? Even Laura, she thought. Was there any reason? Laura now collapsed on her side, Tess watched as a bit of saliva dropped from her lip onto the sheet covering of the bed.

Why remember any of it? The backup at the border checkpoint, the long lines at the immigration office, all the People in Flight who passed through the office, that came and sat and talked and walked away, that loped down the hill to the water or up to wade through the sea of tourists and protestors on Istiklal. Through the marches that were constant and could be about anything: against the internet ban, against domestic violence, football supporters, gay pride, education reform, opponents of Kurdish separatism. Bullhorns and posters and the riot squad parked in front of Galatasaray, a line of young men in blue, with shields and helmets, waiting for something to happen.

Like everyone in the neighborhood they walked by the white tanks on Taksim Square, the soldiers with their limp kalashnikovs, thinking nothing of it. Until the IMF protests that grew and grew until Tess and Laura walking together were pushed back by the crowd, the side streets filling with kids running, chased by cops in helmets. The whiz of rubber bullets something Tess had never heard before.—Come on, Tess.—Laura pulled her down the hill toward Çukurcuma, the hoarse shouts of young men on all sides. They stopped at the entrance to a çayhane to avoid being stampeded. The door pulled open from behind them and they practically fell in into the room, men shouting *gaz! gaz!* as the hissing canisters could be heard landing on the cobblestones down the hill. A tall man with a scar down his right cheek pushed the door shut, went to close the ventilator and lock the door. There were only two other men in the teahouse, one white-haired and dressed in a kitchen apron, the other with thick glasses and a newspaper. The cook beckoned to them—Back here—and indicated Tess and Laura should walk through the narrow kitchen and out a rear door into a courtyard just big enough for a plastic table, a few chairs, and an ashtray. It was protected on all sides by five- and six-story buildings. Just a patch of sky above, where a single cloud sat motionless. The cook had brought the teakettle and scarface went in for cups. They served tea to their two unexpected guests. They sat drinking tea, the men asking where are they from, how they like Turkey—Where is it more beautiful, here or there?—complimenting their Turkish. Finally the rattle of backgammon dice, the sky darkening over the surrounding buildings, scarface laying a hand on Laura's shoulder. Many thank yous and please come again and they were out the door with clean rags covering their mouths even though the teargas had long since dissipated. The smiles of the men before Tess and Laura turned to head down the hill, now dropping the rags and feeling the fall air, the neighborhood already returned to its nightly rhythms.

It wasn't until after Laura was gone that Tess really did get teargassed, fighting through a gang of cops and kids and women and pots and pans, the clank and clatter of the canisters through the shouts. The searing pain in her eyes increased until tears ran and the tears were like acid on her skin. Tess ringing the bell of a friend of a friend, someone she hardly knew, but whose apartment was right here—Please, please, please—and who let her up in order to dab her face with a cloth dipped in milk—This is what we used to use, the friend of a friend said—and it didn't even occur to Tess to ask her where or why. Instead the woman dabbed the cloth with milk and placed it on Tess's face and sang to her quietly, as if she were trying to put a baby to sleep. Tess could feel the tears subside but then her nose started to run and the snot running down her face was like acid, too.

By then Laura was already back in the apartment in Hell's Kitchen. The news from her mother and her flight home, weeks became months, before Tess visited, her first time in the US in five years. Sitting with Laura in that apartment, going through boxes of photos and letters, looking not only for memories but for things that might be sold to pay medical expenses, then taking a break to sit in the cold sun in the park on 51st and 11th Ave, just around the corner, with the smell of horseshit blowing through because somewhere nearby was the building where the Central Park horses were locked up at night.

A lot of them are Turks, you know, Laura said.

Who?

The horse and carriage drivers. I always walk by and hear them talking.

With that smell of horseshit in the air Laura had explained that she was going to stay home, meaning there, with her mother, whose decline had started rapidly, a cascade of bloodclots that left her bedridden, confused, quickly unable to take care of herself. Laura shook her head in resignation, certain that she needed to stay.

I can't leave her here with nobody, she said. I've been in other people's business for so long, it would be perverse not to be here for her.

Tess would have to go on without her, seeing clients and pushing through process, caseloads and interns and grant proposals.

You'll do great.

Sure, she thought. She knew the job by now, had already been doing it for months. And she had Eren's experience and relative savvy with the authorities.

We'll be fine. Of course.

Tess glanced in at Laura's mom in her bedroom with the TV on mute, then flew back to Istanbul, to her apartment in Aynalı Çeşme, wondering what she was doing, how she would anchor her life now, what would guide her. As the city grew worse, as the fights with the interior minister grew more heated. The cross-border situation with Iraq, with Iran and finally Syria. Thirteen bodies in a field in Kayabaşı. Sunken ships off Chios. Running back and forth between Istanbul and the satellite cities. Meetings in Kayseri, in Van, in Antioch. A weekend conference in Vienna, arguing herself hoarse with a Milanese bureaucrat. Back in the office moving papers, making calls, interviews and requests and donor meetings and protocols.

A break to call Laura, bedside with her dying mother in medical America. Calling and then not calling. Why call? What more was there to say? An electric feeling on the skin and in the teeth. Walking the familiar streets until Tess found herself in front of the teahouse where they had taken refuge those years before. Didn't stop to say hello or enter to sit down and play a round of tavla with scarface.

We had no idea, she said to herself. We couldn't have known it would—

But her phone went off and it was Eren somewhere nearby and yes they would meet and yes another night and tomorrow at the office. Making a note to herself to send an email to Laura to remember that teahouse where they waited out the first of the teargas afternoons.

Tess stood over her now and watched her as if she were molting, as if she weren't exactly human. Laura descending into preverbal existence, writhing and crying out and uttering animal moans and grabbing at Tess's forearms. She was blubbering and her face was taken over by a miserable, inward pout. Disgusting in a way. Ridiculous. And where was Barish? Still eating his plate of food? Did he run away?

Don't be stupid, Tess thought. Stay focused.

Laura moved onto all fours again and backed up against Tess. She reared up and grabbed Tess's wrists and brought them to her hips, pushing forward as if she were trying to use Tess's hands to pry apart her own pelvic bone. She let her head fall back and Tess could see her eyes squeezed shut. A pounding artery ran up the center of her forehead. Her cheeks and lips were limp. Then she fell forward again, pushing harder. Tess felt her own hips respond, moving, trying to keep her balance, those moves written into her body.

Laura no longer part of her daily life. Which went on without her in the office, without her at the last meeting in Antioch, before it was overrun with refugees two years later. Tess could still hop a cab across the border to Aleppo and then catch a bus to Damascus—Uuuuuunnnh—where she sat in a little hostel outside the old city waiting for Max to come down from his mountain retreat.—Aaaarnnnhhh—Pacing the alleyways around Bab Touma, feeling full of sunlight, despite everything. Thinking how calm Damascus was. None of Istanbul's rampant hedonism or Cairo's extreme poverty. No idea what was coming.—Euuuuuuuuugh.—People were courteous, welcoming. Perhaps it was an illusion, but she felt completely safe. She was tucked into a café behind the Umayyad mosque watching the passersby, when two students struck up a conversation with her, amused at her Egyptian accent. They were eager to speak English, and Tess was happy to give them a chance to practice. Both with trimmed beards and conservative haircuts. But what struck her most was their friendship. She considered it, just the way they related to each other.—Here it's bad, they said. There is no chance for us.—They wanted to go to America, whatever that meant to them. Tess was saddened to hear it, but even more at her inability to communicate something about that sadness. She had nothing to tell them that would make them appreciate what they had. I would've thought the same, she thought. How could she explain her half-brother, who had left the clean and affluent suburbs of America to wander the arid peaks of Syria, and who was happy there? How stupid would they think him? She told them: I know it must be bad, but I have a feeling that eventually you'll look back on this period with nostalgia. She huffed to remember. I wonder what happened to them, she thought, longing to be like Laura in America, smelling horseshit. To be like Laura, gone to America to take care of her dying mother, getting to know the smells of the dying in her own apartment, so different from in the camps and fields, the pharmaceutical smells of American death. And then this: new life coming into the world in this ward twelve floors above the streets of New York.—*Tess*, she said over the phone. *I got pregnant.*— The students behind the Umayyad mosque sucking in bitter Bahraini shisha smoke and wishing for America, and Tess not knowing how hard the lesson would be for them, or what they wanted, that last time she saw Damascus, the striped walls of the old city and apartments blocks built on cleared orchards. Walking with Max for a few days, then taking the bus together to Aleppo. A few days of strolling through the souq, finding the canteen behind a Christian church where they could order a beer, stumbling back to an old Armenian house where they could sit on some stone terrace that seemed eternal, the vines and stones and cool breeze of Aleppo that would soon be shot to hell.

Where would those two students be now? she thought. Still in Syria? Armed and radicalized? Or in an apartment in Beirut or in one of the camps along the border. Maybe they did make it to America. And were somewhere wondering if Damascus will be destroyed like Aleppo. She imagined everyone who had left coming back years later and it was like her friends from Sarajevo returning after years of refugee life in Boston or Toronto. Having grown into other people, eyes glued to the television but eventually the focus fades. Life is here, anyway. Not ready to go back. There's other things to do, somehow, until it becomes unbearable. You have to go. Finally to see it, that it was still real, as it is now. That would have to happen all over again.

She and her brother on the Aleppo rooftop, before all that. They sat at a table in the cool breeze, about to go their separate ways, Tess wondering why they were so unmoored and inexcusable.

Why do we do it, Maxwell?

But he didn't know either. She remembered him bone thin and quiet, saying:

I always expected myself to be able to take care of you. But I could never do that. Actually it was you who took care of me.

Tess remembered stepping over the vomit of a girl he'd brought to their apartment in Sarajevo, of his disgusting floor on Attorney St, of his concrete balcony above the rooftops of Belgrade.

If I couldn't take care of you, he said, who was I? Sometimes I felt I had no power at all. But I wondered: maybe there was a way to change things, to take care of something. I wanted to find out what I could do.

Tess thought of her first visit to his tower apartment in Belgrade, Max pointing through the gray-brown rooftops at the last Belgrade mosque, the only one to survive, its minaret visible just a few blocks away. That was before his first trip to Istanbul, where he'd had some kind of epiphany at that Sufi ritual, or so his girlfriend claimed. She would have seen him now and said I told you so.

Max emaciated and calm in the fading afternoon:

Now I find myself in a situation where the exercise of my will is at an absolute minimum. Like my failure opened up and I fell right through it. I'm still falling. And like that I feel things I never felt before. Without any idea what it will bring.

With that, whatever that meant, he left back to his monastery. She followed him to the bus station and he went to his mountain, the pulsing in his brain drained of options.

Alone back at the Turkish border she faltered, thought about turning back, about taking the cab to Beirut instead of Antioch, calling Abim. Perhaps that would have been the time to do it, she thought, then there would have been a chance. Then it would be me rocking my hips like this, with my belly bursting with life. But no, that's only more illusions of control. The flames of inevitability already becoming sweet.

Crack.

The door opened and the lights flipped on, Laura let out a suffering moan to protest the harsh whiteness, rolled to her side and draped an arm over her eyes. Tess registered the muttering of voices. First Barish having finished his food, behind him Nurse Joanne, and behind her, now after a couple of hours, Tess was surprised to see that it was still Dr. Shen.

The doctor smiled at Laura, who lifted the arm off her eyes briefly to look back at her.

Tess collapsed once again into the armchair by the window.

You hanging in there? The doctor put a hand on Laura's forehead.

Laura nodded vaguely. Tess felt her eyes were covered in wax.

Dr. Shen turned away and looked at the feeds of numbers, looking over the shoulder of the nurse, who had taken a seat at the workstation.

Mm hmmm, she said. Looks just fine.

Barish stood behind them, as if trying to understand what they were looking at, but it was just a string of digits and graphs, so he looked away, walked over and leaned on the biohazard countertop.

How are you, *aşkım*? he said to Laura.

The Turkish word hurt Tess's ears, coming from his American mouth. But Laura didn't care, she didn't have the same associations, maybe. She had turned her head to see what was going on in the room, gave Barish a mute smile, then let her head fall back. Tess, from her seat, could see up her nostrils. Flaring and relaxing. The bright white light making everyone ugly.

Okay, mama, Dr. Shen said. I'm going to do a quick examination to check your progress.

Laura scootched over and centered herself on the bed, bent her knees and brought her feet up toward herself, then let each knee fall to one side. The doctor held out her hand for the nurse to apply more of the gel onto her two fingers. Again Tess thought she should be holding a long cigarette. But she reached down and inserted her two fingers into Laura's vagina, concentrating for a second. Barish stood back against the wall with his arms crossed.

Six, Dr. Shen said to the nurse. Minus two, 90 percent effaced.

The nurse sat at the workstation and recorded the numbers.

The heartbeat sounds fine. The baby's doing great. Just keep doing what you're doing.

The doctor stood up, removed her latex gloves, and smiled down at Laura.

If you start to feel rectal pressure, let me or the nurse know, okay?

Rectal pressure? Laura said.

The urge to poop, the doctor said. That'll be the baby's head moving down. Then it's time to push.

Laura nodded and moaned and moved back onto her side, facing the window. Dr. Shen said a couple of words to the nurse, said goodbye, and was gone. The nurse followed her to the door and shut it.

Please, nurse, Laura said, can you turn off the lights?

Of course, said the nurse. And flipped the switch, providing a welcome relief.

Now the nurse stepped next to Laura on the bed. She reached over and began to massage Laura's side and one of her shoulders. Laura responded with a moan, moving her knees and rotating her hips to the left, up and out, up and out.

Come here, the nurse said to Barish, who walked over next to her. See what I'm doing? Don't be afraid to really dig in. You try.

She backed up and Barish moved into her place, working on Laura's hips and shoulder and back. Laura's moans continued along with the movement of her hips. Tess was happy to be relieved of duty. Her arms were practically numb from all of the pressing and pushing.

You might want to try nipple stimulation, the nurse said.

Excuse me? Barish said.

It can help the effectiveness of the contractions, the nurse said. Give it a try.

Barish very gingerly reached over and put two fingers on Laura's left nipple, making a slow clockwise circle. It seemed to Tess that as soon as he touched her Laura began to scream and moan.

Ah, no. I can't. I can't.

Barish backed off for a second but then Laura grabbed his wrist.

Do it, she said. Do it.

And Barish again stimulated her left nipple and she screamed and moaned.

Again the door opened and closed. Tess remained watching from her chair, while Laura screamed and gnashed her teeth, Barish looking down, as if he hardly understood what he was doing, helpless in the face of this wild creature.

The thrashing started right away. As soon as Tess got back from Syria at the end of 2010. There had been desultory marches in Istanbul like always. Plans to redevelop the waterfront, another round of internet bans, though even the prime minister talked about how to work around them. Tess stood at the top of Boğazkesen watching LGBTQ protesters with multicolored signs, wishing them well but expecting little. She heard about the self-immolation of the fruitseller in Tunis—How horrible—but never expected the dictator to flee. When he did, and then when Egyptians poured into Tahrir in January, Istanbul ceased to exist. Life became a blur of unanswered phone calls to Rasha. Tess remembered the tiny protests in Tahrir when she was living in Cairo, so powerless. Fifty students surrounded by hundreds of cops. Now the entire miserable chaotic square was full, where she had dodged traffic so many times to get to Adri's, to get to Laura's in Garden City, or to get to the dreaded Mugamma rising up at the far end, where she went to renew her residence permit. Now the crowd poured in and swelled until the mass of people grew so large it was visible from space. Tess saw satellite images forwarded, liked, bookmarked. And the protests spread beyond Cairo. Factory workers struck across the country. Healthcare workers. Those plump-faced nurses with their signs. Women workers speak out! Scuba divers swam through a reef somewhere, holding signs that read: *Fish Want the Fall of the Regime!*

Tess sat in her office with the feed running, sat in her apartment with the feed running, checked updates and posts and arguments and celebrations. Watching and checking on the roof with Eren as Omar translated for another person in flight.

When she finally got through, Rasha's voice sparkled with euphoria—Something's happening, finally!—Tess was pained not to be there. Like when Katarina called from Belgrade after they'd driven a bulldozer into the RTS building.—Go! Smash!—But no, this was different. Egyptians, Tess thought. How exactly it was different she couldn't say.

Adriana, when Tess got ahold of her, held her camera up to the window so Tess could see Tahrir. The same crowd that was on all the feeds. Those tarps and flags and men and women standing and sitting and jumping and speaking. Hands in the air. What she had seen from space was now a vast abstract mass just there down the street. She could hear it out Adriana's window over the familiar horn-honks of downtown.

Look, Adri told her. The square is like a single body. No one is going anywhere! I've been down there singing. Sitting in the middle of the square and singing. Yoooh!—Adri set down the camera and Tess could hear her banging on the wall with a stick or a spoon. When she appeared again she was flushed, in hysterics. She held up her hand, curled her fingers into a fist.—One body, she said.

But the next days brought gunshots, rocks, horses and camels. Cops releasing prisoners with crowbars and knives, telling them to run amok. Cops idling in front of NGO offices, carrying out computers and cabinets full of papers.

They couldn't even start their car! Rasha laughed, but Tess felt only her rush of determination and optimism.—And in the square, now, men wait in line for tea. Imagine. Egyptians have learned to wait in line!

Rasha laughed again and returned to the fray. Until Mubarak

made his speech, his sinister face saying *I too was young once.*

Fuck you young or old! they shouted.

And after February 11, when the government fell, Rasha was in tears and confusion but joyous. Tess felt the shock and elation, too. Milošević, she reminded herself, fell not because he was a genocidal dictator but because he lost all the wars he'd started. And it had been what, ten years? This was different. None of the Egyptians of her generation were even alive before Mubarak's state of emergency. Their entire lives had been a state of emergency.

No more of that, Rasha said. How will we survive?

The part of Tess so certain that the students in Damascus would rue the day, for a moment, was quiet. We had won, whoever we were.

Tess watched footage of the celebrations on repeat. She watched a man bend down, kiss the ground and let himself fall, roll onto his back and look at the sky. When he got up he looked into the camera and said: *We will walk this earth among lovely flowers.*

All around him people wept, swung their arms, jumping and screaming. Explosions and horns and the clack-clack-clack of bullets.

A single body thrashing on the ground. A nerve that once touched swept from here to there to there, like a reaction in the ankle that leads right up to the hip, the shoulder, the neck, the ear. Until you felt it, you didn't know that pathway was there.

Now in the hospital room Tess felt she would swoon, just remembering all that. She had never sucked in so many pheromones or hormones or whatever they were. Laura's body was a swollen ball of fumes, a planet emanating human reproduction. Tess saw it from space like the protests. Against all her pessimism, here it was: the continuation of the species. This is what it smelled like. Covering over the rubbing alcohol scent of the ward was this prehistoric smell of the human species desperate to go on.

How long had it lasted? she thought. Days? Was it even a week? How long before it all turned. The first assault was that very night, she remembered. By the time she talked to Rasha, so euphoric, there were already reports of the CBS journalist assaulted and raped. Something had already shifted, they just didn't know. How could they have known? Demonstrations that became elections that became crackdowns.

She thought of Rasha a year later:

Listen to these headlines: *Constituent assembly approved despite secular outcry; Islamist views spark secular outcry.* Me and Yousry are going to start a band called *Secular Outcry.*

But that period passed, too, as fast as it began. The men who'd cheered and protected everyone in the square, waited patiently in line for tea, now crouched in alleys, afraid. Facemasks and hoodies and shaved heads and scarves over mouths. All the terrible stories Rasha would eventually tell her. The assaults, the massacres, more assaults.

And it was everywhere. From Morocco to Jordan to Yemen to Bahrain. Then the violent reprisals began in Syria, and she had no way to call Max, alone in his mountaintop. It was not the sorrow and heartbreak of defeat that she felt, but the metallic nerves of anxiety. She hated him for being unreachable like that, willed him to call, to appear at her door.

Max's last letter was propped up on her bookshelf, and when it fell off unexplainably one night she tossed and turned until morning. She dreamt of him, dreamt of Abim, even. She felt as if the blood and bone had been removed from her and she was just a shirt and a pair of trousers, run over by some armored vehicle, like what she'd seen happen outside Maspero. Emptied of spirit completely, so quick had these reversals come.

So when the protests started in Istanbul, too, when crowds gathered in Gezi to protest the cutting of trees, the construction of another needless mall, and Eren was day and night in the square, old women on balconies banging pots and pans, cheering when the Beşiktaş hooligans went rampaging through the neighborhood in a stolen backhoe, with all the gleeful chants and scrambles, Tess was alone in her feeling that it would never work. She was happy to let Eren and his friends in, when they showed up with Coca-Cola and lemon and bandanas, the tools for fighting teargas and pepper spray on the alleys.

May he step on a wet bathroom floor wearing socks!

They laughed and drained bottles of Angora wine together before stumbling further down the hill.

Tess watched them go, shaking her head, thinking: There will be no breakthrough.

They wanted to breathe the air and love and celebrate, to relish all the monsters and miracles of the city, the country, that spit of land between the fertile crescent and the Balkans, as another place that everything passed through. But there weren't enough of them. And their celebrations made her bitter and alone, now with the office full of Syrians. With every application and family reminding her of the revolutions hijacked and dashed. Thinking it would all only get worse until the fade-out comes and the solitary philosophers of extinction walk the sterile halls of the hospital, wondering what to do now that the parasite has been eradicated.

Aaaaack, ahhh, eeeennnh.

Laura winced again and this time she squeezed her eyes so tight Tess thought she would burst a blood vessel. God, she looked down at her friend, it's like an aneurysm. How many women had a stroke or a heart attack at times like these? It's like dying. A real moment of crisis. But her face is so flushed and beautiful.

I guess it was worth those few days of laughter, she thought. All night in the square together. Hanging books from the tree. That feeling that we might change everything, be together in a new world. It didn't matter that it would never happen.

She was wrong to doubt it. Eren had been right, even if it did him no good.

When he got truncheoned and ended up in the German Hospital Tess had gone to see him every day. He was hopeful, couldn't wait to get back to the barricades. And when they released him he did go right back. But as the protests faded he came to her at the office with his face pale and blank. He sat in his own office for a month. She could see that his focus was gone. He couldn't find it in himself. The elections came and went again, solidifying the ruling party's power, and everyone she knew fell into despair.—There's no place for us in this country.—Eren came to her and told her of his decision. He needed a change, he said, or at least some time to think. He was giving up the job, giving up his apartment, and going to stay in Kaş for a while with his patron, the elderly Englishman who had helped him so long ago.

A place where I know I'm wanted, he said.

When he was gone Tess remembered his enthusiasm, his joy during those days of protests. At least he'd had that, she thought. He was right to do it. Next time I'll join in. I'll yell and sing until I drop. And when I drop, I won't care anymore.

Barish was kneading Laura's hips and shoulders the way the nurse showed him, but Laura was starting to get to her feet.

The movement of planets, curses and hexes.

Tess, Laura was saying. Please you do it.

Really? Tess couldn't help saying.

Yes, Laura nearly shouted. Come on, please.

Tess got to her feet, feeling like an old woman showing the young ones how it's done. Laura was wincing and growling as she moved her feet onto the floor. She pressed the button to raise the bed higher, folded her arms and buried her face in them, muffling the screams she was making.

Please, Tess.

Barish backed away, making room, and Tess made her way behind her, put both hands on the sides of her hips and pressed as hard as she could, despite her aching muscles, the increasing feeling of weakness.

Yes, Laura said. Yes.

Tess had no choice but to continue, feeling Laura's body pressing back against her and then softening, listening to the screams and cries she made into her folded arms, inhaling the loamy explosions of pheromones. The air in the room was liquid. Barish was helpless, silent, now it was him in the green plastic armchair, or squeezing the wet cloth from the ice bucket, laying it over Laura's back.

Yes, she said. No.

Tess pushed and pushed, feeling exhausted and angry and almost used. Laura's selfish back glistened with ice water and sweat, streaks of red where she had lain against the mattress, drops of fluid still leaking from between her legs onto the padding on the floor. Tess moved her body to the side and pushed again as she felt the pressure wracking Laura's abdomen. She nodded her head to Barish to tell him to come over.

Together, Tess mouthed. Let's do it.

And moving to the side so he could squeeze in next to her, threading an arm between Laura's back and Tess's chest, they both pushed on Laura's hips, shoulder to shoulder, awkwardly intertwined.

Aaaaaarrrggh.

Laura let out a gurgling scream, the pain seeming to get worse as they pushed.

No, she said. No.

When the next contraction came on Tess watched Barish move over and plant a kiss on Laura's mouth. The slurping and movement of cheeks and tongues and necks. ·

The room felt claustrophobic and Tess took the opportunity of Laura's distraction to get up and walk to the door. She heard Laura call after her—Tess!—when the door opened and the light burst through, but she didn't listen, just headed out to the hallway. Let Barish deal with it, lover that he is. Let them deal with it together. She wasn't going to be around to raise the kid, anyway. They were going to have to be together with no help from her.

Ahh, she shut the door behind her, so happy to be in the hospital corridor again, that change in the ionic charge somehow, the whole air less tense. She felt the knot in her belly and walked down to the other end of the corridor. There must be a bathroom somewhere, not the one in the room. If she could just pace the halls for a second, empty her bladder, she'd be able to go back and keep on with this, all the pressing and pushing.

Everything okay, hon?

Nurse Joanne came down toward her from the nurse's station. Her frowsy hair and eyes peering over the red rims of her glasses. It took Tess a second to find her breath.

Everything's fine. Just came out for a second. Is there a bathroom?

The nurse led her around to the double doors at the entrance to the ward, right next to the waiting room at triage. Tess remembered herself there some hours ago. I've aged since then, she thought.

Nurse Joanne pulled up an ID strung on a lanyard around her neck and placed it next to the brown plastic box on the wall and the double doors swung open.

Just there, the nurse said, indicating the bathrooms on either side of the elevators.

It occurred to Tess to take the stairs, to wander through the halls of the hospital, open random doors, see who's there. Who's in here? Hey, how's it going? No, just stopped in to say hello. Perhaps she could strangle a nurse and take her scrubs and her ID, hang the lanyard around her neck, the reading glasses. She'd wander slowly through oncology and radiology and hysterectomy until she got down to melancholy, hysteria, and haunting.

The bathroom felt good, cool and quiet. She stood in front of the mirror and looked into her face, gauged the redness of her eyes, the blemish on her left cheek. God, look at this face, she thought. No wonder I'll never have a baby.

She walked to the stall, grabbed some paper from the roll and wiped down the cold toilet seat, unbuttoned her trousers and sat down on it. She crossed her wrists and let them fall between her knees, her neck stretched forward and her hair fell toward the floor, her same brown hair. She exhaled and felt the urine release from her bladder, the gurgle of water in the basin. There was a sexual sting in it, an ache. She pulled a bit of paper from the roll and wiped herself.

What do these chemicals do to you? she wondered. Fantasies of wild women with distended tongues, slashing their mates and carving up their bodies, eating the liver, insulin dripping from their chins, the true women, what she really was.

She stood up and pulled her pants around her hips, looked into the basin for a second then pressed the flusher, watched the soggy paper spiral down. Down it went, and Tess stepped out of the stall and into the empty tiled room. Back in the hall, she walked the other direction away from the labor and delivery ward. There were still pictures of babies on the walls, of children standing in fields. Doctors and nurses running here and there.

But what a relief to be out of there for a second. She grabbed her elbows and pulled her arms to herself under her breasts, felt the pressure of her own belly. She puckered her lips and wrinkled her nose, closed her eyes and opened them.

She was still there.

She began to walk, the wrong way into the postpartum ward, away from the infant screaming somewhere off in the distance.

Barish didn't know if Laura's face was beautiful or horrible, but when he kissed her he felt muscle power and breathed in the smells coming off her, which were perhaps disgusting, but even so, were fucking sexy. In the way that only something repulsive can really get you. Woman in raw state. Laura's eyes pressed shut and her mouth hanging open. He saw his pawprints on her breasts. It was good to be alone again for a second. Laura opened her eyes now, and they were red and wet and undulating.

You're doing great, he told her.

She gulped down air, hardly a moment between contractions. They were just coming and coming.

I can't, she said. I can't.

Yes you can.

My mother, she said. I want my mother.

She's gone, Barish said. And he moved to stroke her hair, lift the strands out of her eyes.

She's like a madwoman, he thought. That's the only way I've ever known her. Maybe only one week, the week the old woman was in the hospital, when we had the place to ourselves, and she wasn't knocked up yet. Only then, he thought. But she was crazier than ever.

Laura pulled back her lips, exposing her teeth, her lips curled into a snarl. A growl sounded long and low. Almost like a purr. That was still her somehow, the week without the aid. The old woman in the hospital. The two of them together, that drugged exhaustion. On the floor, on the sofa, on the balcony overlooking the Hudson, smoke rising from distant chimneys in New Jersey. Laura knocking over furniture, that wild laughter when she was about to come. But somehow he knew what to do, how to keep hold of her, just on the edge of losing it and she would snort and chortle and swallow like a drowning horse. Then the old woman was back and they had to keep quiet, had to keep still in the next room, so different.

She didn't make it, Laura said between blubbering inhalations. She never made it. I missed her.

It was hard to tell if those were tears from her eyes or just water dripping down from her hair and around her contorted mouth. Her cheeks bunched up and her nostrils flared. Her breasts that had been so perfect were now huge, with broad, aggressive areolae.

Aaauuuaaarrrrnnh.

The sounds were emanating from down in the bottom of her throat. What to do with this woman? This wasn't even a contraction. She was just a blubbering mess. Almost want to climb on top of her, pin her down and ride her, hold on tight as she bucks and flails.

Why? she moaned. Why?

What's happening, lover? Where are you?

Where's Tess?

I don't know. Maybe she went to the bathroom.

Fuck her, Laura said. Then she began shaking her head: Why?

She broke into a sob for a second. She was losing it. Where was everyone? Would he be able to do this himself? Meaning deal with her? He saw her hands grip the mattress, the low sounds still coming from her mouth. This same body. The bubbling and gurgling in the funerary apartment on 10th Ave. This same body that had taken over his mind. He was leaning over the mattress, now, with his hands on either side of her hips, watching her as she moved from side to side.

One of her hands found his wrist and she gripped him, now gripped both wrists and tried to pull herself up, or pull him down to her. He put all his weight into his hands so as to become steady and solid.

Fuck I hate this, I hate you, I hate all of them. I don't want this anymore. I don't want I don't want I can't aaaeeenghghghgh.

Barish tried to breathe easy, hoping she would follow, or at least be calmed even slightly.

Say something! she screamed.

He knew whatever he said would be wrong.

Tell me something!

You're doing great. Just breathe. Hold onto my wrists. That's good.

Fuck fuck fuck. I'm going to kill her, I'm going to kill her.

Barish hardly heard the sound of the door open but Laura somehow did and jerked her head around.—Tess!

I'm here, her friend came up to the other side of the bed.

Laura still had her grip on Barish's forearms, wouldn't let up even the slightest.

Tess, she said again.

Barish and Tess made eye contact for the first time in hours. He saw her worn and hardened. That kind of boyish, bony body. Sharp hips and shoulders. Something soulful and intelligent in her face. He might like her, after all. He never found himself with that kind of androgynous woman. So different from this one.

Tess, Laura was raving. I'm going to kill her, she repeated again through her blubbering sobs.

Tess stood next to her and put a hand on her forehead.

Don't kill her, she said, and started laughing. Why should you kill her?

And Laura started laughing too, or somehow a laugh crept through her growling and hiccupping.

I'm going to kill her, she said, half-laughing, half-crying, shaking her head back and forth.

Don't kill her, Tess said. Or go ahead. Maybe you should kill her.

I'm going to kill everyone.

Then a wave came on and her words disappeared into another sound. Barish was tempted to back off, but he couldn't. She still had him. She clenched and screamed and he thought he could see the squirming explosive movement inside her body, her hips forward, her pulsing cunt speaking to him.

Is it gonna happen?

It's gonna happen.

Is it gonna fit through?

It's gonna fit through.

Am I gonna be all right?

You're gonna be fine.

Are you sure?

Yes.

It's gonna happen?

Of course it is.

It's gonna fit through?

It's gonna fit through.

Are you sure?

I'm sure.

I want my mother, Laura called. I want her to be here.

I know, Tess said. But she's not.

Barish was rubbing her shoulders behind her and Tess was in the green armchair, facing her.

How can I do it?

You can do it.

Are you sure?

I'm sure.

It's gonna fit through?

It's gonna fit through.

Tess stood up and came closer, draped her wrists around Laura's neck and put her forehead against Laura's forehead.

It's gonna happen?

It's gonna happen.

It's gonna happen?

It's gonna happen.

Laura felt the contraction strengthen again.

It's gonna happen.

It's gonna happen.

Laura's words started to disappear into the abstraction of pain.

I can't. Oh, oh. I can't.

You can.

I can't. Ayyyyy caaaaan't.

You can.

Pleeeease.

Yes. Tess said.

Pleeeeeease.

Okay.

Okaaaaaay. Laura spoke through gulps of air.

Okay.

Okaaaaaay.

The war in Syria dragged on, only getting worse. Tess had heard nothing from Max, had no way to check on him. Pacing through her apartment in Aynalı Çeşme, her only option to send a letter with the Turkish post. Did she even expect an answer? Him in his mountain refuge. She had no idea. Weeks passed and she had no idea.

Finally he called from Beirut. From a little apartment at the edge of Bourj Hammoud.

I'm with a girl, he said, stifling a laugh.

My God, Max, you could have sent word.

But he was overcome. He was in another world, far from her:

They came and got me from the cave. One of the novices came up, told me the father had been expelled from the country, they were trying to run the monastery themselves.

Tess pictured rough brown robes on the arid slope. Max stepping unshaven out of his cave, gathering his things and following:

I came down and found the place practically deserted, and everyone nervous, not knowing what was going to happen. I didn't even have a chance to say goodbye to him. He was already gone.

Tess wondered what the father had meant to Max, really. The booming voice he'd described. Who had welcomed him, who had understood his need to be there:

They said he'd headed east, was going to try to cross the border into Iraq. I asked the novice what he was going to do, and he said he would to stay put with the other two. Just the three of them up there.

Everyone gone. I thought I better go, too, so I threw my stuff together, which is nothing really, at this point, and I went to Damascus.

Max ducking through the striped arches, the alleys of the old city where they'd walked the year before:

I looked for my bookseller friend but his shop was closed up. I called his number and talked to one of his family members, and they said he was in Beirut, gave me a number where I could look for him there. I got a ride to Beirut.

Coming over those mountains, finally the sea in the distance:

I got to Beirut and felt crazy, like I should spend all my money right away, so I got a room at the Mayflower Hotel, not far from Abim's. It was full of journalists and UN people.

Richard Bright would be there, too, Tess thought. The whole swarm converging.

Max was breathless, going on:

There was a little swimming pool on the roof, he said. And I just sat there on the roof. I felt like I sat there for days. I was so overcome by the drastic change, by the speed of the change.

You could have called, Tess said, keeping a lid on her swifter emotions. I was going crazy.

I know, I'm sorry. I thought to call, but then I didn't. I don't know why. I was worried too. I don't know how to explain. I went out into the street, I walked through the city. I hadn't seen Abim. I called the number to try to find my bookseller, but there was no answer. So I walked across the city. I walked through the center and over to the other side, and I sat down in the first bar I came to, a little place at the bottom of the Christian quarter, and I sat there, and I started drinking. My first drink in months.

Tess could see his eyes start to spiral, all the solitude unleashed in a gush of madness:

I sat there all afternoon, and there was a girl in the corner reading a book, and when she got up to pay she was fishing in her bag for her wallet and dumped everything out on the ground. Pens and papers and everything all over the floor. I wanted to help her and I knelt down to pick up something and I knocked my head against hers, and she fell down on the floor and so did I, and we both started laughing, and I don't know, I guess I paid her bill and left with her.

Them stumbling out into the streets of Beirut. Tess clucked her tongue like a Balkan grandmother as he kept talking:

We walked out into the sun. And I was already drunk, and she just turned to me and said: I'm a mess. And I asked her to come with me to my hotel and she said fine, and we went to the Mayflower and sat up on the roof. I felt so lightheaded I don't know how to explain. We were up on the roof and the sun was setting over the sea in the distance. I didn't know where I was or what was going to happen. The last of the money I'd saved is almost gone. I was there with the girl on the roof.

Tess remembered the elation in his voice when he said all this:

For three days she didn't go home. And we sat on the roof and ate breakfast in the breakfast room. We watched the breakfast room fill with journalists. There was one, very august looking, who just couldn't get the toaster to work. She sat watching him press his toast down, but it would just pop back up.

Max giggled like the idiot he was:

I had to get out of the hotel. So she brought me to her place, in Daoura, at the edge of Bourj Hammoud.

And what now?

Well, he said. I called Abim, I talked to him. He thinks he can find something for me. I don't know what. Dealing with the situation. It's ridiculous, but I guess that's the only thing for me. What else can I do?

His nervous laughter put her on edge. Amid all that, the inevitable onslaught of refugees, the familiar panic, contractors regrouping, sat-phones lighting up, more organizations and operations and clustering and team building and press conferences, the pain and confusion and trauma that would be entrenched for generations, for centuries, to hear him for the first time in years so delighted.

What had changed in him up in that mountain? What had become of her mournful and sentimental half-brother? Now he was like this?

You should call Abim, he said. I'm sure he'd like to talk to you.

And hanging up, Tess thought about it, and perhaps riding Max's strange mood, hesitated, finally sent a note to Abim.

He wrote back right away to say he'd call her in an hour.

Laura was gripping the mattress with her fingers, her face red and purple. Barish was standing in front of the biohazard counter at the foot of the bed. Sweat circles grew at the armpit of his t-shirt. Nurse Joanne was talking to Laura:

You can feel it. I know you can feel it. You're right on the edge, hon.

It's too much. It's too much.

I know, hon. But you're just there. You can feel the tightness. That's your cervix. That's the feeling.

Laura was squirming to the right and the left. The nurse had lowered the back of the hospital bed, trying to make Laura lie flat, but she kept trying to move one way or the other. The nurse handed Barish the ice bucket stuffed with handtowels and leaned over to look Laura in the eye.

Listen, hon. I know this sounds crazy, but you're going to have to move toward the pain.

Aaaaaaahhhh.

Barish was ringing out a towel to place on her belly.

You want to resist, to run away, the nurse said. But don't. Listen to the pain, and move toward it.

Laura cried and sobbed and then went quiet for a second.

The more it hurts, the more you listen.

Tess, Laura said.

And Tess, so tired, hardly sat up, but her eyes came to life at the sound of her name.

I'm here, she said.

I'm going to leave you for a few minutes, the nurse said. Then I'm going to come back with the doctor. Okay?

I caaaaaan't, Laura said.

You're doing great, hon. Just do what I said. Listen to the pain.

The nurse reached over and cupped a hand behind Barish's neck. Tess watched her turn and leave, like a gnome or a phantom. Her frowsy hair still in place. The light sliced into the room as she opened and closed the door.

Tess, Laura said.

I'm here.

Look at me, Laura said.

I'm here.

Look at me, Laura said.

Tess pushed her hands against her knees and got to her feet. Outside she could see the light starting to turn. Dawn over Midtown, just unveiling.

Look at me, Laura said.

I'm here, Tess said.

Laura was still turned away from the window, so Tess had to move around Barish to get to the other side of the bed.

Barish pulled off the towel and stood useless, looking down at the side of Laura's belly, still stretched as tight as ever, her skin discolored. The half of her face that was visible ran with tears and snot. She opened her eyes and stared at Tess for a second, with a possessed gentleness in her gaze.

I need to get down.

Okay.

Tess, I need to get down.

Okay.

Tess stood up. Barish came around to get her other side. Together they helped her to the floor.

She let out a huge, reverberating yell. Tess thought she heard the instruments rattle in the echo.

We got you, Barish said.

His face was blank, his treebark voice a dry croak as if he had been screaming, not Laura.

It's coming, Laura said. I can't do it.

Laura turned around and pushed against the bed, backing again against Tess, who was reaching around to try to raise the hospital bed.

UUUUUnnnnnnnnaaaaah.

Barish steadied her as Tess managed to raise the bed.

Maybe you should go tell the nurse to come back, Tess said to him.

He nodded and ran to the door. Through the galloping heart she heard it open and shut behind her.

Tess, Laura said.

I'm here, Tess said.

Look at me.

Tess squeezed her hips as she had done all night.

Aaaaah! Laura shrieked. Stop stop stop.

Tess pulled her arms away as quick as she could.

It hurts it hurts. Laura was breathing again in gulps.

Tess stood helpless. What could she do?

I need to go to the bathroom, Laura said. Help me.

Okay, Tess said.

Tess stopped first, and reached over Laura's shoulder and unplugged the cables from the heart monitor, threw them over her friend's neck and shoulders. In the ensuing silence, she took her under the armpit and helped her stand up. Laura turned and faced her now and threw her arms around her neck and stuck the top of her head into Tess's face.

Oooo ooo, aaa aaah, Laura said.

Tess struggled to steady herself, not to get tripped up in the cables.

To the bathroom, Laura said, motionless.

Tess didn't know what to do, then began to step backwards away from the bed. Laura, her arms still around Tess's neck, her head bowed forward, followed her steps. Slowly, together like that, they moved across the room. Laura groaning and wincing. Tess moving backwards, struggling to stay on her feet, supporting practically all of Laura's weight. When they got near the door to the little bathroom, Tess moved Laura around and walked her backward.

Here we are, she said. Bend down. I've got you.

Laura began to bend at the waist and the knees and Tess struggled to stay underneath her, gripping the doorjamb with one hand, until Laura's ass made contact with the toilet seat.

There, Tess said. That's good.

She uncurled Laura's arms from around her neck and made sure she was steady.

Tess, Laura said. Can I just stay here for a second?

Of course.

Tess took a step back, catching her breath. She couldn't believe she'd managed not to drop her. Laura was seated on the toilet in the dark, her head bent forward, her hair falling forward. Now despite her huge belly she looked small. Tess could hear her crying and moaning. She stayed for a second, then turned away and went back to the room, which was empty now. Light was starting to come in through the window, and soon they would lose the comfort of darkness.

Abim's warm voice echoed in her memory as she waited, impatient until the stupid sound of Skype rang. She clicked to accept the call and there he was, his hair almost entirely white, but even through the pixelation his face so familiar. She could feel her stomach drop. She thought of Max in his strange girl's apartment.—I'm a mess.—What was happening?

How are you? Abim asked.

Fine, she said. And you?

Stressed, he said. I'm sure like you. There's a lot going on.

She had nothing to say about that.

Are you happy in Beirut?

Of course, he said. I'm completely at home.

Max says you may be working together.

Yeah. He seems to be doing well, Abim laughed.

Yeah, I know, she laughed along with him, and felt that warmth rise up in her.

You know, she hesitated. Maybe there's something for me there, too.

Abim was silent. She watched the movement as he turned his head to the left, as if in slow motion along the surface of the screen.

You want to come to Beirut? he asked.

Maybe, she said.

She could see him, or imagined she saw him, weighing the possibilities, what to say, what it might mean.

I don't know, he said. I don't know if that's such a good idea.

She was silent. She felt the acids in her stomach start to bubble. What had she been thinking? A fool, once again. But then the desolation made her calm, somehow. There was no way back.

Yeah, maybe you're right.

The window to that life had shut and vanished. She could hear his voice, tinny and compressed through the speaker.

It's good to talk to you, he said. I'm happy to see your face.

You too, she said. But I should really go. I have to get back to work. I just wanted to say hello.

Hajde da se čujemo, he said in awkward, fading Serbian.

And she clicked the program shut, with the fragment of that language they'd once shared ringing in her mind.

Laura had come home, she thought, and if she had a home somewhere, she'd go there. But there was no place to go. She could only stay where she was. She left her office and walked back over the hill to Aynalı Çeşme and closed herself up in her apartment and cried. For the first time since she'd come to Istanbul, since the ruins of the revolution in Egypt, the war in Syria, the gas and barricades, Eren, the onslaught of the displaced, her solitude, absolutely without hope. She lay there on her bed on her back, tears streaming down her cheeks, thinking: Take me, I'm yours. Useless. Rip me apart, I have no use for this. She sobbed and convulsed and all the loneliness and confusion bubbled up and covered her, washing and stinging until somewhere within or beyond all that her good and hopeful heart shone through, her crazy optimism and love for the miserable world, for the light and the faces, the sound and the stupidity, for the dug-up fields and ditches full of bodies and bombed villages and mules and malls and teahouses and rubber bullets and beheadings and vile politicians and her family and the little house she grew up in behind the art museum, this world, this country, me, whoever, all of it drained onto her cheeks and ears and down onto her purple pillowcase, her nose running with snot and her throat swollen, choking and letting go, until all that was left was the softness at the bottom of herself, the meek and careful lovingness that enabled her to get up, to look out at her tiny slice of a back garden, and see it with cool and gentle eyes, to fill the teapot and listen for the whistle, to pour and steep and sit.

The pale, thin air of the morning came into being as Laura cried and moaned alone on the toilet. Tess stood in the middle of the room, very old and very alone, everything she'd ever been and thought coming into her at that moment, helping her friend, suspended in that aspic, the webs from her fingers reaching to Kansas City, to Beirut, to the Balkans and Istanbul and Cairo, all the places where the people she'd cared about were, to the versions of herself she'd left behind, to all the transient and confused. She felt light and strong, standing still. What to do? The question she always asked herself, whenever it wasn't quieted by the immediacy of someone else's need. Like tonight, but now she felt it slip from her. She was isolated from everyone, and could feel the outlines of her person, the reach of her life, and there was a solidness to her, standing there. The bitterness that so often rose up within her now settled. She walked over to the hospital bed, still cockeyed and jostled. The cotton padding still soaking up Laura's body fluids, the thick silence without the sound of the galloping heart. Through a kind of ringing in her ears she noticed Laura's moans and cries breaking through, laboring there alone on the hospital toilet. Laura alone, too, after everything, after all the years and borders and friends and lovers, about to plop her baby into the toilet. The baby not knowing where it would end up, still hovering in undefined possibilities, neither here nor there. It might be a whitewashed house in Upper Egypt. It might be a muddy field along the border with Kosovo. It might be Research Hospital in Kansas City. It might be a ceramic tile floor in Cuernavaca.

Or it might plop into a porcelain throne twelve floors above Hell's Kitchen, getting on into the twenty-first century.

Tess breathed out, long and slow, and felt herself sag slightly in exhaustion. She put her hands on the mattress and rested. The baby warmer didn't look as menacing now in the light of the morning, its insect eye still watching her. A benevolent alien, like the succulents on the Marmara islands, sending reports from the throat of the world.

OOOOHHHUUUNHHH.

A long, heavy moan came from the back of the room. Tess turned to check on Laura, but as she got closer the door from the hallway flew open and nearly bashed her in the forehead.

What's happening? she heard Barish's voice.

Come in, Tess answered, stepping out of the way.

Laura was hunched over on the toilet, cables loose around her neck, her elbows on her knees, legs open, moaning in a low, animal way.

I'm here, Tess said. But Laura didn't respond.

Barish pushed his way through and behind him Tess could hear the footsteps of others.

Where is she? came Dr. Shen's voice.

Here she is, the nurse said.

Tess was aware of them standing behind her and turned to look.

Is she already pushing? the doctor asked.

Do you feel it? the nurse asked. Do you feel it bearing down?

Laura let out another moan.

Even if you feel the urge, the nurse said, try not to push just yet.

Let's get her back to the bed if we can, the doctor said. It will be easier to examine her.

Tess backed away and let the nurse come closer, coaxing Laura up off the toilet. Barish was pacing back and forth in the middle of the room, taking up too much space. Tess stood waiting for him to notice her, to stop so she could get around him. She could see the tension and alarm swimming on his face. She reached out and took both his upper arms for a second and squeezed them. Her arms were incredibly strong by now. Her exhaustion had slipped away. She could have lifted him right off the ground. He turned his eyes toward hers, then shut them and began to nod, slowly, with his eyes shut, and she could feel the trepidation coursing through him. She dropped his arms and moved around the foot of the bed, back to the green armchair, and watched shards of sunlight break through the buildings, drawing stark yellow lines on the opposite wall.

Now the doctor was backstepping, the nurse and Laura coming toward her.

Tess moved out of the way and the nurse brought Laura to the bed. Laura again collapsed forward onto her arms and buried her face there, moaning and swaying her hips.

We just need to get you up onto the bed for a second, the doctor said.

The nurse kept a hand on Laura's back, and with the other felt around for the button to lower the bed. As the bed came down Laura's face was forced up out of her arms. Tess could see her now, crazed and red and strung with greasy hair. Like she'd just popped out of the sea.

Now, the doctor said, indicating that Laura hop up onto the bed.

Laura threw one knee up and began to climb. Tess jumped up involuntarily. It looked dangerous. Laura seemed unsure of what she was doing. Tess grabbed Laura's shoulders and steadied her. Laura looked back, but at that moment she had no idea who Tess was.

The nurse tried to guide Laura onto her back, but Laura went the other direction, got on all fours with her face toward the pillows at the head of the bed. She let out several steady, gruesome moans, and dropped her face into her arms, her ass in the air facing Barish and Tess.

It's okay, the doctor said. I can examine her like this. Joanne, please raise the head of the bed.

The nurse reached over and pressed the controls again, and the top half of the bed, with Laura's face pressed into it, began to angle up toward the ceiling. The nurse grabbed Laura's armpits and jostled her until Laura could rest her arms and head on the pillow at the top of the bed, her back straight. The doctor ran a hand down her back, as if she were a horse or a dog.

I'm just going to check on you, okay?

She slid on another pair of latex gloves. The nurse squirted gel, and again she slid her cigarette-holder fingers into Laura's vagina. She paused for a second, feeling for whatever she was feeling for, the opening of the cervix, Tess supposed.

Yes, she said to the nurse. She's fully. Plus two.

The nurse leaned in and spoke quietly into Laura's ear.

You're ready to start pushing, hon. This is the time. Okay?

UUUhhhhMMMM, Laura responded.

Nurse Joanne must have called for reinforcements, because the door to the room flew open and a new team rolled in, pushing some kind of surgical table into the center of everything, its green cloth cover topped by a tray and a jostling rack of metallic devices. Laura pressed her head against the pillow and her ass faced the room, now crowded with people.

No more changing and growing, Tess thought. She was here with Laura and the baby was really coming. And when this was all over, in a week or even less, she would go back to the life she alone had made. Through blindness or refusal or whatever it was. Turkish Airlines and back to Aynalı Çeşme, walking over the hill to the office, to the stream of seekers, without Laura, without Abim or Max or even Eren.

If you could just gather your things, the nurse said, and get them out of the way.

She watched Barish look around in confusion, until he saw his jacket on top of the biohazard counter. Tess noticed everything on the floor, the bag she'd packed with Laura the day before. Everything looked weeks old, and now in the light of day, she felt like she was looking down from a great height at the room now filled with bodies, green smocks and white aprons, scalpels and scissors and forceps and pliers. From her seat in the corner she leaned down, picked up her jacket, the blue bag they'd packed, and held it on her lap.

Nurse Joanne saw her.—You can just place everything there on the windowsill for now.—Tess looked to her right, got up and shoved everything there where the nurse indicated.—Just so there's a clear space between mama and the baby warmer, for when we're ready, nothing on the floor.

Tess stood up, her hands free now, and looked around. Outside, dawn was moving into day. The doctor must have been on duty ten hours or more, as long as Tess had been here. She sought out the doctor's face, looking down as she pulled on latex gloves again. The new nurses helped her place surgical covers on her clogs. Dr. Shen was like a prizefighter, cracking her neck, heading into the ring.

Tess among these smells and instruments, the sleeves and pokers of the ward. She felt completely insignificant. A facilitator, something to be looked past and stepped around.

With that thought, alone among the instruments, something struck inside her, and and with that, out flowed the death wish that had always pulsed through her, what she'd tried to dissolve in the pain of others. Her thirst for meaning exploded over the skies of Kosovo and Cairo, evaporated above the gardens of Aswan, and her memory was wiped clean. No one needed anything, really. She might as well do whatever she wanted, whatever that was. Take a drag on one of Bekir's big crumbling joints and jump off the Kadıköy ferry to swim through the submarine paths along with the last of the Bosporus dolphins.

Laura was still facing the wall, her ass in the air, waving and moaning. Nurse Joanne was next to her again, one hand on her sacrum, speaking into her ear, low so Tess couldn't hear what she was saying. She saw her mouth form a circle and blow, showing Laura how to breathe, Tess imagined, how to stay calm as she was ripped apart.

Dr. Shen pulled a mask over her face, clapped her hands together, and was ready to go. Joanne was still whispering to Laura. One of the new nurses turned to the knobs and dials on the metallic square on the wall marked Skytron, the controls of a torture device with the image of a person and arrows in four directions, a knob below that indicated a range from *low intensity* to *high intensity*. The unknown nurse punched a button and a bright light turned on above Laura, like a spotlight, shining down onto the bed, lighting up Laura's swaying behind, her head still moaning in the other direction.

Joanne, the doctor said, let's turn her around.

Yes, doctor, the nurse said.

The other nurses nodded and said something to Dr. Shen, then the whole crew headed for the door.

Thanks very much, the doctor said.

And then they were gone. A relief, Tess thought, to have the room less crowded again. But there was the table of tools they had brought, shining in the morning light.

Okay, the doctor said.

The nurse brought Laura's arms up onto her shoulders and began walking her slowly in a circle. She nodded with her head to Tess—Why don't you help me, hon.—And Tess came forward, took one of Laura's arms. They held her like that for a moment, on her knees, upright, her belly forward, pointing toward Barish, one arm over the nurse's shoulder, one arm held by Tess. Her face was straight up toward the ceiling, drilled by the dry white light from overhead.

WWWWHHHUUUUUHHH.

Waves were wracking Laura's body. The doctor stood back, letting the nurse and Tess get her into place. The nurse, again with her head, indicated they should lay her on her back. Tess didn't see how that was possible. Barish came forward and took her by the hips, steadying her. Laura's armpit was in Tess's face, and she had no idea what was going on. Screams and struggles. Whose hand was that? Finally Laura's ass came down on the bed, her knees shot out to each side, her back and shoulders lay on the raised portion of the bed, and her belly pointed up, directly under the spotlight.

Tess stood back, caught her breath. The nurse was bent forward, dismembering a portion of the bed. With help from Barish, now, she yanked out a pair of footrests, foot holsters or something, another element of the torture device. The bed had become a gynecologist's table, Tess realized, and a shiver went through her, all those sparkling tools. The nurse was fitting Laura's feet into the footrests and lifting them higher, so her knees came closer to her armpits. Dr. Shen in her facemask was still standing back, observing and waiting.

Huh huh huh huh huh huh.

The nurse placed a hand on Laura's forehead.

That's good. That's good. We've got you.

Now, mama. It's time to push that baby out, Dr. Shen said, stepping forward.

Is it gonna come? Laura said.

You're doing great, the nurse said.

Is it gonna come? Laura said through her gasps.

You're on your way, the nurse said.

Now, the doctor said.

Barish and Tess looked at each other. Tess thought that they must have exactly the same expression, the same concern and anticipation and exhaustion and mystification.

Come here, the nurse said, indicating Tess.

Tess stepped up to the side of the bed.

I want you to take one leg—

Ah ah ah ah ah eeeeeeee, Laura interrupted, panting and screaming.

The nurse let Laura's leg go and smoothed her hair off her forehead.

Just breathe, the nurse said.

When the intensity passed, the nurse took Laura's left leg under the knee, and indicated Tess do the same with the right. She moved around to face Laura, so Laura's foot was pressed into the side of her belly.—Hold it like this, she said to Tess, so she can press into you. And she supported Laura's calf and her knee with her hands.

Tess felt the sole of Laura's foot press into pelvic bone, toes curling into her liver.

Laura's eyes were opened and she looked at all four of them in terror and confusion.

Now, the doctor said. I want you to take hold of your legs with your hands.

Laura reached for her knees, but the nurse guided her hand around the outside, so she could grip her own thighs from the outside.

Pull your legs toward you, the nurse said.

Laura looked back at her, the same look of fright on her face.

I, I, I, I, I, she said.

When you feel the pressure, the doctor said, pull your legs toward you and push. Do you feel a contraction coming?

Laura closed her eyes and cried out. Her legs tensed. Tess could feel the pressure against her, could see her fingers digging into her thighs. The doctor stood between Laura's legs now, and Barish stood behind her, watching.

Move into the pain, the nurse said. Move towards it.

Oh oh oh oh oh oh, Laura said.

Let it come, the doctor said. Let it come.

Tess looked down and saw the breathing and pulsing of Laura's vagina, purple and swollen, full of blood. She saw it grow and somehow open, turning outward from the inside, her whole vagina turning inside out, the huge lips seeking and quivering, a plant looking for light.

UUUUUUNNNNHHHH.

Not like that, the doctor said. You need to keep your mouth closed when the contraction comes. Don't let the air escape, okay? When it comes I want you to hold your breath and push, push like you're going to the bathroom, push everything out.

Another wave started to move through Laura, and she tensed her biceps, pulling against her thighs, like using a weight machine, her arm muscles tense and bulging. Her face more and more purple, her body surrounded on all sides by the nurse, by Barish, by the doctor.

UUUUNNNNHHH, Laura said.

The doctor placed a hand on her belly. The numbers in the feed were extremely high now, over 200.

Okay, the doctor said, when it comes again I want you to breathe in, and then try not to make a sound while you push, okay? Keep your elbows out, curl up around your baby, okay?

Laura was panting, color draining from her forehead. From purple back to scarlet. A single vein or artery through the center of her forehead, pulsing.

I'm going…I'm going to… Laura said through her gasps.

You're doing great, the nurse said.

The doctor, the nurse, and Barish all turned toward the meter. The numbers had fallen back to double digits, but they were climbing again.

I'm going to place my fingers inside you, the doctor said, and show you where to push, okay? There, she said. Do you feel it?

And as she said that, Tess could see an ooze of shit push out of Laura's ass. The doctor removed her latex-covered fingers, which were dripping with pinkish fluid, and the nurse stepped over to wipe it away with the pads that had been placed under her. A cloud of the smell rose up and hit Tess in the face.

That's good, the doctor said. Just like that.

Laura was shaking her head to the right and to the left, her tongue out, saliva out the side of her mouth. The nurse was dabbing her ass with the pad, moving the pad to the side, dumping it in the biohazard container, laying out another as a contraction came on.

Now, Dr. Shen said, I want you to hold your breath and count. One, two, three, four, five, six. Just like that.

Tess felt Laura's legs press into her side, her kidney or her liver, crushing her organs.

One. Two. The nurse was counting again.

Laura closed her mouth and her eyes and pushed. Tess cradled her ankle and pressed back with her body, pushed Laura's leg back against her.

Three. Four.

That's it, Dr. Shen said. That's it, that's it.

Tess could see inside of Laura to where there was a tiny strand like a filament that connected the inside of her left temple to her left jaw, and from her jaw to her shoulderblade and down to the arch of her left foot. She understood that it had always been there. The pounding in Laura's head, her impatience. It emanated from this delicate strand that was at the core of all Laura's desperate movement, her exuberance and anger and fear.

Laura's body now stretched out to breaking, having given up all hope, her bones fracturing, her back tearing, her eyes popping, her heart bursting. Somewhere within that, behind her shrieking and her oblivion, Tess could sense that the delicate strand had broken. When she cried now it was not from the pain, it was from whatever unverbalizable knowledge came with that breaking. What she was as a living being, what could be seen only in light of the snap of that subtle strand, what it was and what it wasn't. For that moment Tess too was both herself and no one, a tissue of pure abstraction, inscrutable and bottomless, as inarticulate as the black of an eye. Experience would teach her nothing. The rest of her life. The child. It had nothing to do with it. She was a bucket of flesh, a flash of light, a code, an emergent spark mistaken for a woman.

Laura began to scream, and Tess could feel the screaming, too. It was a rush and a wash and a divergence. All the cells in her body responded, and it felt wonderful.

Seven. Eight.

Here it comes.

Tess looked down at the little blue bloody mess coming out of Laura's body. Right below her, gripped by latex gloves. A tiny misshapen bulge. Was that the head?

Nine. Ten.

Take a breath, Dr. Shen said. Let's go.

A spring or a ting or something. The air or the light or another burst of odor and chemicals.

Come on, come on.

Laura was pushing, tears streaming down her face. Barish's eyes were headlit.

I see it! he said. I see it!

He was like a little baby.

That's it, the doctor said. One more.

Tess looked from Laura's face to the doctor, and then down at Laura's body, and yes, she could see it. The head. The bulge she had seen was just the beginning, then the whole head came out, enormous, and awake. She saw its eyes open just like in Sasida. It was really a baby. Goo-covered and deathlike. Was it dead?

One more, one more.

A shoulder and then a goo-covered arm and another and then: plop. The thing slid out into Dr. Shen's latex gloves.

It was day by now, and the instruments shone in the morning

light. The bed, the windows, the smell of shit and birth. The baby's eyes blinked. It was alive.

Something about the baby's wrinkled head reminded her of Omar, the translator, his wrinkled brow and sad eyes. Tess pictured him standing on the roof of the office overlooking the straits, considering the world as created by the lowly bureaucrats of the divine. Here came another to be checked in, assigned a satellite city. So small.

A little boy, the doctor said.

Tess had never thought about it. A boy? But there he was. All the noxious fumes of war and conflict and stupidity, boredom and ugliness. A dangling little baby penis. When she finally took a breath, her head filled up with helium and exploded. She was weightless and completely forgotten, absorbed into the vents in the ceiling.

Hummmmm.

Dr. Shen pulled the baby up, cord spilling off to the side, and held him toward Laura, placed him on her belly. Laura made a hiccupping sound, then another, and then tears streamed out her eyes. Tess could feel it coming over her, too, as she descended back into her body. So exhausted. Uhhhhhh. She looked over at Barish and he was tearing up too. Everyone was crying at the birth of the baby. Hello world. All the morning light in the room shimmered and came to a stop.

Ting.

Out of that silence emerged a sound: a quick, almost low sucking sound. *Fwuhhh.* Was that the baby? Tess looked down at him. Yes, it must have been. His lungs opening. Now she could see the chest moving in and out as he started to breathe.

Nurse Joanne handed a couple of white plastic clamps to the doctor, who stuck them onto the cord.

Tess could again feel this body she had, her heartbeat, purple and silver shapes that surrounded her hips. What she had squeezed into Laura left open this singing part of herself, and it was still there, despite everything, even now as she aged, as she accepted everything. It was there like a shining metallic sphere that was singing, ringing like a bell, maybe, a gong that shook through her, that emanated from her, that penetrated the walls of the hospital. A ringing soaking singing sound, swishing like the toxic juice inside the lead weight between her breasts, uniting once again in the center of her body, a sweet and open spot that was something beyond her, this limited life she had always struggled against, that opened into everything she still had to learn, that would guide her, that would take her back, unbelievably, to where she was and would go. She would continue, insanely, without knowing why or where or anything.

Do you want to cut the cord? The nurse handed a pair of scissors to Barish, who was wiping the tears from his face.

He cut the cord without a word. Laura was still crying.

Uuunnnh, she said. Another one.

And out of her body slid another blob of flesh and fluid.

That's good, the doctor said. That's your placenta.

The nurse took the organ in her hands and slid it into a bowl on the rolling table. A heap of tissue, with folds in it like a brain. The doctor was dabbing and wiping at Laura's body. The nurse handed her a needle.

I'm going to give you a small injection, she said.

Laura and Barish were both fastened onto the baby, who lay silently, breathing. Tess felt faint, and stepped back next to the green armchair, looking down at Laura's lower body. Red and purple and huge and open and exhausted. Completely cut off from the world above her waist. The doctor bent over, handed the needle back to the nurse and began to suture.

Just a little tearing, the doctor said. It's just fine.

It was like a bomb had exploded, Tess thought. A world of shredded flesh and dripping fluids, lonely and defenseless. A massacre. A field of bodies. Dr. Shen, tiny and focused, worked steadily away like a field medic. Laura and Barish with their son had no idea what was going on down there.

Nurse Joanne reached up to take a hold of the baby—Just one second—picked him up and placed him on the baby warmer, where he lay on a pad under the insect eye. Barish was looking at Laura, who was staring straight up, at nothing.

Dr. Shen checked the baby's breathing, took measurements. The nurse squeezed some ointment into his eyes so they were gummed up and blind, and placed the baby back on Laura's belly.—Here you go. His lungs are clear. He's a beauty.

When Dr. Shen was finished she peeled off her latex gloves, threw them in the container.

I'll be getting off now, she said. But I'll come check on you in the postpartum ward tomorrow. Congratulations!

Laura and Barish looked at her. Tess said nothing. Barish said thank you, and then she was gone. The door pulled shut and Tess found herself standing next to Nurse Joanne.

Could you give me a hand? the nurse asked.

Full of helium and expanded in all directions, Tess followed the nurse's instructions, helping to lift Laura's legs one last time, so Nurse Joanne could slide on some white mesh panties and insert a very cold white thing inside, like a frozen maxi pad. Tess looked over the terrain of Laura's body, ravaged and exhausted, the white mesh over her blotchy, reddened skin.

Tess, Laura said looking up. I'm hungry.

The hallway was strange and the elevator was strange and the huge open hall of the entranceway was strange, but when she stepped outside the morning air was cool and soft and welcoming. She didn't recognize anyone in the Skotos Diner. The waiter from Larissa must be home sleeping by now, she thought. Every night here at the base of the hospital. Birth and death and birth and death. She ordered food for Laura and sat drinking a coffee while she waited. The warmth and familiar bitterness of bad American coffee. She held her face over the cup, let the steam warm her eyelids.

Now I can go, she thought. I'm free.

Oxygen and helium rose from her hips to her chest and her neck and her brain. She was a windsock flapping at the edge of a carnival. The waiter brought the food all packaged up. Tess bought a few other coffees and some dry, stale bakery items and walked out cradling the paper bag like a child.

It's over, she thought, and felt hilarious. The sun was bright over Manhattan. Another beautiful October day. Like a year had passed since yesterday, since she woke up next to Laura in the big bed on 43rd and 10th Ave, Laura's contractions, the elevator, Mrs. Lefkowitz, the taxi, the hospital, triage, everything. But now it was over. Tess felt a hundred pounds lighter and a hundred years older. Not older in a decrepit way, more like she'd died and been reborn into her same body, the same age as before, but with one more life behind her. Shed a skin, or been relieved of an obligation. All she thought of now was the bed back in Laura's apartment waiting for her. She stood again in the lobby, then rode up the bright, ridiculous elevator to the twelfth floor. She got to Laura's room, and found the door open. There was only a woman in green scrubs cleaning up.

Is this yours? the woman said, pointing to Tess's bag on the windowsill.

Tess nodded, and the woman handed it to her. She struggled to put the strap on her shoulder without setting down the bag of food.

We've had a bit of a backup, the woman said, so they went ahead over to postpartum right away. It's just down the hall. Ask at the desk there and they'll show you in.

Tess stood mute for a second looking at the room, all cleaned up, as if nothing had ever happened. The baby warmer in the corner, waiting for another specimen.

She turned and made her way to the nurses' station, and a nurse walked with her to the postpartum ward.

Laura Valerio, Tess said.

The receptionist checked for the room number and pointed down the hall.

The door was ajar, and she could see Barish in the dimness of the room, seated on the end of Laura's new bed—Hello?—and she drew the door open letting in the light of the hall.

Laura was placid and pale but also glowing. The baby was squirming peacefully on her chest, pink and purple and very small. She had done it, Tess thought. A champion. And Barish looked slightly green, somewhat sickly, but very pleased. They were all swallowed in the chemical glow. The child was the only thing that was real, though that in itself was unbelievable.

Tess, Laura said. Come here.

Tess stepped in, handing the white paper bag to Barish.

I brought food, she said.

She felt Laura's and Barish's eyes on her as she looked down at the baby, neither of them seeing her, but seeing the baby through her eyes. Very proud, she thought.

I'm going to your place, Tess said. I've got to get some sleep.

Laura just nodded, still with a smile.

Did you give it a name? Tess asked.

Not yet, Laura said. But we should think of one.

She let out a laugh. They all laughed. The baby squirmed in its place.

Or not, Tess thought. Maybe they shouldn't give him a name. Tess would certainly have remained like that, if she'd had the choice, referred to by a grunt or a nod of the head.

Here.

Laura handed him to Tess. Tess took him, gingerly, bounced him in her arms. The feeling of skin like wet paper. Gummed-up eyes. Everything very small.

Goo goo goo, she thought.

I'll take him.

Barish reached for the baby and Tess handed him over.

I'll come back later, Tess said. I'll come check on you.

Laura just nodded, and Tess turned away.

Not to be her or it or anything. That would be the best, Tess thought as she left the room. She closed the door behind her, not completely but so it remained ajar, as it had been when she'd approached. The family in there, the child breathing in the half-light.

The traffic on the avenue was calm as she walked alone back to Laura's building, into the straight lines of the brick and concrete high-rise. She stepped inside and collapsed onto the bed, among the cool crumpled sheets. Sounds came in through the open windows, traffic on the highway, the insistent rush of cars and trucks. The bedroom dark and cool at the back of the apartment.

She could feel the weight of her own body now, finally, the backs of her calves and her ass and her brown hair playing against her shoulders, the lines around her eyes, the clenching in her intestines, until she breathed out and let it go, that tiredness, and sank into the mattress as the heaviness came over her. The room was thick and syrupy, wavering: the furniture, the unpacked boxes, the painting in the hall of the sepia fruitstand, the empty coffee cup from the morning before, the unscrubbed plates in the sink, her unanswered emails, the schedule of work next week when she got back to Istanbul, the caseload waiting for her, the new media dump, the Turkish ministers dressed like Ottoman pashas for a costume ball, airstrikes against the Kurdish positions in Iraq and northern Syria, repercussions of repercussions.

She pictured her little apartment in Aynalı Çeşme, the slice of sun that beat on her tiny garden, the iron chair, the neighbors beating their rugs, the kids playing on the street, the blare of the call to prayer in the morning, the incessant movement of the boats on the straits, the sunken ships in the Marmara, the heavy heads of her clients and colleagues, the buses and cabs and construction sites and closing notices, the bowls of soup and bottles of oil and pickled onions and candied olives, her brother and her ex and her other exes and future exes and her increasing solitude, afloat between them, curving east along the water, to Beirut, to the mountains between Damascus and Homs, to places she would never go, to this darkened bedroom above Hell's Kitchen.

The ravaged landscape of Laura's body and the dark and cool room where she left them, fine and complete, a new family, whatever they were, and now she could let go of that, too, and just sink into the mattress. The heaviness grew until it began to bubble and carbonate. The swirls in her hips and the juice in her chest all boiled away and the density of her bones lessened until the empty space at their center expanded. Her eyes sunk into her skull and her cranium and brain were like the placenta in the bowl, folds and flesh to be slopped into the biohazard trashcan. The cool dim light of the bedroom wavered, permeating the emptiness of her bones and her head. Her memory and desire extinguished, and the bed lay empty without her.

Acknowledgments

To the ex-Yugoslavia, where I came of age, to Anja and Nadja and Miran, Tina and Naida, Amra and Igor, to Bojana and Biljana, Žunić and Nala, Tričko and Bane and Djurdja and Nikola, Nathan and Ana and Arta and Marcel and all those families, to Vlado who published my first book. So many hosts and friends who helped me in Cairo, to Farrah, to Yasmin and Omar and Ahdaf and Rafiq, to Malak, to Maha, Yasser, Ian, and Haytham. To Andy, Borda, and everyone downstairs in Budapest, to los Ilić, Bass, and Kashefi, and to my extended family there. To Ceren in Istanbul, to Deha and Yasmine and Edward, to the lost tribes of Schleifers and Mullinses and Alpays and Boblar, and Miss Kate. To Achille and Refqa and Raluca and Antonnis in Berlin, to Marianthi who took me north. To Darius for the much-needed connection. To Profesor Guzman in the San Rafael, and to Maestro Cons and El Gran Cesar in the mountains of Morelos, and to Hamdi. To Lucy, and los Hanley, to Ayana and Cynthia wherever they may be. To Dan V and Lili and Fanni who read early versions, and to Aron too. To Jace and Rocio. To Rico, Madhu, Monique, LaTasha, Clayton, Katherine and Kavitha, to Meline and Alex, Mert and Defne, to 409 and the ICC, all who make me at home in New York. To Sean, Shelley, and Shibi. To Marco and Daff, Suleya and Ayele. To Khaled and Martina and Walid. To my brother Raphael and a monumental Skøl! to Kristina and Sabina whose heroism instigated this story (along with Compact Evie). To CD and all the Bradys. To my grandparents. To the everlasting Jeanne and Jack and Sarah, Ayla, and Mete. To my students at City College and to all the Hunterites and GC-ites, especially Claire and Colum, Joan and Wayne for joyful support. And very much to Ammiel and Jess who brought me to Rescue, and to everyone at Rescue, especially Hilary, who worked every word. And to Domjan, szerelmem. Locura!

Biography

Brad Fox's stories, articles, and translations have appeared in the *New Yorker*, *Guernica*, and the Whitney Biennial. From 1996 to 2011 he worked as a journalist, researcher, and relief contractor in the Balkans, Mexico, the Middle East, and Turkey. He teaches at City College in Harlem.